# Haunting Suspicions


By
Kate Richards

Copyright © 2016 by Kate Richards
ISBN: 978-1-68361-032-8
Cover art by Fiona Jayde

Published by Decadent Publishing Company, LLC
Look for us online at:
www.decadentpublishing.com

## ~What Others Are Saying About
### *Haunting Suspicions*~

*The well-written scenes and details capture the imagination and the quaint little town full of captivating characters ensures that the readers come back for more* ~ Amazon Reviewer

*Delicious ending to satisfy any hunger* ~ Amazon Reviewer

*A very quick read that leaves the reader breathless. Every which way the reader turns, there is another layer of mystery, suspense, and intrigue, and the loving is, of course, not left out! The chemistry between Alden and Orlena is enthralling and has you rooting, against all odds that Alden's "haunting suspicions" lead him to love!* ~ Amazon Reviewer

# ~A Note from the Author~

Dear Reader,

I hope you enjoy my story of paranormal activity in a Western ghost town. My husband and I spend time every year prowling the towns of Northern Nevada and the Eastern Sierra and we love hearing the locals tell us the ghost stories and legends, so here is one that didn't happen...but wouldn't it be amazing if it did?

Thank you so much for reading my books. I hope you'll drop me a line and let me know how you like Haunting Suspicions.

***Kate Richards***
Katerichards09@gmail.com

# Chapter One

The woman brushed past Alden and into the crowd, leaving behind a fragrance of violets that went right to his head. Her lithe form filled out the period dress she wore and the bustle...okay, so he was an ass man. How much of what he focused on belonged to her and how much to the wire or whatever frame under the many yards of brown fabric covered with sprigs of pink flowers and leaves? Normally, he wouldn't have noticed the print...but when it swayed over a bottom like that?

He lifted his cup then grimaced and tossed his cold latte into a faux whiskey barrel printed with the words *Goldland Township, trash only*. What else would he put in it? Clearly not bottles and cans. A fake beer keg stood nearby marked *Goldland*

*Township, recyclables.* He chuckled. How appropriate for the late 1800s. Still, he had to admire their ecology-mindedness. Not many of the ghost towns he debunked made the effort. While he'd been distracted by ironic wastebaskets, the object of his lustful interest had left his field of vision.

Peering over the heads of the people along the boardwalk, he searched for a sign of the desert rose, but she'd disappeared. Her ensemble made it likely she was a local, though, participating in the ruse that had brought the town back from near extinction to a thriving tourist mecca. Over the past few months, every ghost-hunting show had arrived and left with footage of "real" hauntings. Even one or two teams who usually could be counted on to debunk the lies and cheats that people employed to draw attention to themselves, for whatever reason.

Like many small towns in less-populated areas, this one had suffered from a lack of economic opportunity, leading all its young people to leave in search of jobs and higher education. It had been, according to his researchers, in danger of drying up and blowing away before the Indigo Princess appeared.

But the good people of Goldland had better beware. On the day of the full moon, the production crew for *Not on My Watch* would arrive to film the monthly hijinks which made the town so popular. They would begin their stakeout right after the gala parade scheduled for nightfall the next night.

So he had the rest of the day to occupy himself with undercover investigation. And he wouldn't have minded a little chat, maybe grabbing a drink with the pretty lady with the sable brown hair and the interesting bustle—in the name of research, of course. Perhaps a little of the Strong charm could get her to spill the details on what everyone was up to.

Unknown to the devious denizens of yet another deceitful town...Alden Strong, host of the program, had already arrived to do some snooping. There were bound to be citizens he could get chatty in the saloon with later on. By the time the actual vans with the logo on the side drove into town and the cameras rolled, he would already have the scoop, and it would be just a matter of showing the public that there was still no such thing as ghosts.

Or real fortune tellers.

Werewolves.

Vampires.

Fairies.

Or effective get-rich schemes.

But in this case...ghosts.

As the sun crept below the horizon in a ball of red-and-orange fire, the traffic began to thin out. The lodgings couldn't hold all the tourists at this time of the month. From the news footage he'd watched, many people still stayed in a much bigger town nearby, where there were a couple of casinos and more hotel rooms—but remodeling on several mid-nineteenth-century buildings promised more accommodations soon. A gaming license was also rumored to be in the final approval stages for the saloon.

He didn't mind people getting ahead, but he despised them using the feeble minds of gullible fools to do it. Not that they didn't deserve it.... Wasn't the world interesting enough without spooks and aliens?

He pulled a small tablet from his pocket and made notes on the buildings he passed. A mercantile, a saloon—spilling Sons of the Pioneers-type cowboy music—a rock shop advertising local ore...and across an alley, a two-story schoolhouse, freshly painted and, judging by the period-looking but clearly new playground equipment outside the door, still in use. He paused when a light flared in one of the upper-story windows. Who would be there so late in the day?

He had some ideas. It could be a teacher with papers to grade or a janitor or....

Perhaps someone working on a project they didn't want the tourists to know about? A new ghostly surprise for the full-moon night? If so, he needed to take care. The double front doors were closed and, even if he had wanted to be seen there, probably locked. Not worth taking a chance on testing. Making a quick left, he strolled down a steep street alongside the building until he came to a side door. When he had a lull in the pedestrian traffic on the main street, he slipped into the shadows of the overhang and reached for the handle. Yes, it appeared locked was well, but, to his great luck, ajar.

He pushed inside and found himself at one end of

a long, dark hallway lined with lockers with a steep stairwell at the other end. The door clicked into place behind him, taking with it the streetlight's glow. The flashlight app on his phone helped him navigate along the wooden floors of the basement level, testing each step for creaks and cringing when he found one. But, though he paused, nobody from upstairs came rushing to see who was there. In fact, he had time to scan the pictures on the walls hanging in the gaps between banks of steel lockers. Framed class portraits with dates as old as the 1860s, sepia and tintype gave way to full-color photos of modern kids in T-shirts printed with sayings inappropriate for prime time television.

The stairs were remarkably quiet, and he reached the top of the first flight undiscovered as the last of the light faded from the sky and the moon tipped into view through the big window on the landing. But he had another set of stairs to go, and it was at the other end of the hallway.

No class photos adorned these walls; they were lined with display cases stuffed with trophies for sports and scholastic competitions and a bulletin board featuring entries for an essay contest entitled *Do You Believe?* He slowed and held the phone close to read the title on one: *The Indigo Princess, I believe!* Were they even brainwashing the kids? The essay had been graded with a big red A. They rewarded delusions?

Or perhaps the contest was for the benefit of the tourists.

Discounting the bulletin board and its contents, he strode through a typical school hallway—even if it did hold the musty scent of over a hundred years. Reaching the stairs, he climbed again, wincing at every creak, marveling that no one appeared to challenge his presence, and arrived on the second floor.

A stream of light emerged from a door halfway down this hallway, and he stopped, listening. How many people were in that room? Had he found the control room? Very clever to hide it in a working school. The paranormal effects he'd seen on the many ghost hunting shows filmed in the town would have to be the result of some spectacular electronic genius. No simple orbs and electronic voice phenomena that could be translated as *Go away nowwww* by eager ghost hunters, or simply static.

Full-body apparitions and poltergeists were the order of the day...or rather the night.

The gorgeous spirit of the Indigo Princess, lingering in the saloon once a month, drew thousands, all of whom seemed to share the beliefs of the essayist.

The silence of the building, combined with the close, unmoving air sent unease up his spine. Not fear. Alden Strong was never afraid. But, still, it didn't take ghoulies and things that went bump in the night to cause harm. A townsperson whose very livelihood was threatened by his presence could do just as much damage—more—than any imaginary haunting.

He crept closer to the light, switching his phone to camera mode and wishing he'd brought a real camera with him, but he'd not dreamed it would be so easy to find his way into the vipers' nest. Just a few feet away from the door, he heard a scuffing noise and raced forward, camera at the ready....

A strain of music began, something classical,

violins and flutes, and a soft voice singing words he couldn't quite make out. An angel, an aria, the scent of violets just touching his nose.

The woman from earlier, or was she even real? He peered through the crack between the door and jamb to see her seated at a desk as old as the rest of the building, singing softly and marking something on a sheet of paper. A stack rested to her left, a shorter pile to her right, and she was...grading papers.

A single lamp on the desk lit her in a spotlight and cast the rest of the room in shadow. Her deep-brown hair was piled on a head bent over her work. Her collar rose high, a bit of lace touching her throat matched at the wrists of her long sleeves. The dress was fitted over her breasts like a second skin, but everything was covered, and somehow so much sexier than the tight tank tops and short shorts of the women on the street below.

Transfixed, he watched as she finished one paper, moved it to the right, and lifted another from the stack on the left. And then another...for how long, he couldn't say. What century had he fallen into where the schoolmarm looked and smelled and sounded like this? He could stay forever, lost in the lulling of her voice.

He could be a rancher, coming to court his sweetheart, to take her out in his buggy and watch the moon rise over the desert landscape while coyotes howled and small creatures scurried. The cooling breeze blowing tendrils around her rosy cheeks and her soft, dark-brown eyes peeking out from under a bonnet.... Would she have worn a bonnet at night?

Hats didn't matter, but her eyes did, with their long lashes. Her full, moist lips parted as she sang. His fingers itched to open just one—the top one—of the row of tiny buttons that ran from her waist to just under her chin. To bare her throat and taste it there under the scratchy lace. To open another and one more and nibble at the hollow there, sucking gently at the skin. She would moan and arch her back, inviting him to go on until, finally, he would grab the fabric and rip it open to her waist, unable to wait any longer to bury his face in her cleavage, surrounded by the scent of violets and warm woman.

The notes of a jazz ringtone jerked him into reality. She pulled a cell phone out of a drawstring bag, lifted her head, and froze, rosy lips parted in an O that turned his cock to steel.

No, he wasn't in the 1800s; it was 2015, and he was an electronic media maven himself, clutching both a tablet and his own phone.

She waved him to a seat in the front row, and, opening the door, he did as she bid and he folded his length into it. Alden waited while she discussed the next day's events with someone on the other end and hung up. Amazed she didn't then call 911 or even tell her friend she had a creeper, he licked his dry lips and kept his focus on her.

After a moment, he realized the classical music was actually an obscure 1980s rock ballad, and it issued from an iPod docked on the credenza to her left. Next to a closed laptop. The lamp was neither oil nor gas but the far less romantic, energy-saving, and modern LED version.

The tattered fragments of the dream dissolved.

The woman leaned back in her chair and arched a fine, straight brow. "Another tourist lost his way? Or are you something more?"

He swallowed hard, struggling for words. Words

he never had trouble finding. "I—"

She lifted a hand. "No, please, let me guess. You were looking for the ghosts and saw my light, so you came up here to see if I was a dead schoolmarm still working away at ghostly assignments into eternity?" Lifting a ruler from the chalkboard tray behind her, she tapped it on her desk, and a whole new set of fantasies flitted through his supercharged mind. Lust filled his veins.

He shook his head.

"You followed me here in hopes of getting an A in...something?" Her deep-brown eyes with an exotic tilt held sternness, but the corner of her mouth twitched, and he broke out in a sweat.

Sucking in a breath, he straightened and returned her regard. "I think I could earn that grade." He met her stare with one he hoped held all the fantasies she'd already engendered. If she was only the local schoolmarm, free to grade papers right before the full moon instead of stringing wires and hanging sheets— of an electronic nature—then perhaps she was a simple townswoman, uninvolved in the shenanigans, and he could make a move. Most of the locals dressed for the full moon and the days leading up, but surely only a few knew what was really going on. The rest were probably just too happy at the tourist dollars to question anything or perhaps knew only parts of the puzzle. Often those made the best accidental informants. Was she one of those? "If you would like to test me."

Who knew he had a thing for historical romance—or historical lust?

"Really? In reading, writing, or 'rithmetic?" Her tight dress showed every breath she drew in and let out, and his eyes rested on the curves of her high breasts for a moment before returning to her face.

"Animal husbandry."

She dropped the ruler and broke into a laugh. Which made her breasts heave even more. If he couldn't charm her into a one-night stand, walking was going to be uncomfortable for the foreseeable future.

# Chapter Two

Orlena Estelle's giggles slowly stopped. She took in the man before her, a lock of brown hair falling over his forehead just short of one of his dark-blue eyes. An unusual shade, almost indigo, that gave drama to his square jaw and full lips framed by five o'clock shadow. He wore a black T-shirt tucked into designer jeans and a pair of worn Tony Lamas that said, while he might be a tourist, at least in footwear, he was no poser. Though the elements said *casual*, they fit as if tailored for him.

His biceps strained the short sleeves, and she followed the dark hair sprinkling his forearms down to broad hands with long fingers currently flexing on the surface of the too-small desk. He might have a hard time getting out of the one-piece chair and desk, designed for a ten-year-old, which would keep the entertainment going.

She rarely paid attention to the tourists, beyond courtesy and playing her role, but something about him intrigued her and drew her out of herself.

Overall, he was the best-looking intruder she'd had stumble into her classroom in some time. Which probably explained her flirtatious behavior. She'd be on the carpet if Tex Smithson found out. Their pride alpha seemed to suffer under the illusion that she would be his eventually. Not in this lifetime.

She mentally compared the two. Tex's lean form, feline and graceful, held the attention of most of the younger women who came along. With his dark-gold hair and amber eyes, he had a reputation as a good lover, one she thought he'd bought into himself, and his air of entitlement irritated her every time he came near her.

No, she had no interest in him, and neither did her cat.

Unlike her visitor, whose easy smile and more muscular form made her and the cat both want to purr.

Tired of stress, strain, and the general nonsense of the past few months, she gave herself permission to enjoy a little company. "So, what's your name, cowboy? That is...if you are a cowboy?"

He shook his head, and that lock of hair shifted just enough to say *I don't need hair product to look this good.* "Not a cowboy, but I could imagine myself a rancher here to call on the pretty schoolmarm." A wicked grin lifted his lips, and her heart thumped. "You can call me Al."

It had been a long time since she'd let herself get naked with a man. She knew every single fella in town like a brother, most of the tourists were far from appealing, and her one big love affair in college had taught her how dishonest a man could be when he wanted to get into a woman's...pantaloons.

But her dry spell didn't have to last much longer. Why should she deprive herself of a little casual pleasure? Men certainly didn't.

Standing, she moved around to lean on the front of the desk. Seemed as if her guest liked the 1870s-conservative look she employed when doing her part to draw tourism.

"Nice to meet you, Al. What brings you into town in the middle of the week? Cattle drive?"

He lifted a little, but the desk held him, and he dropped back to the seat. She suppressed a smile, watching his hands flex on the desktop as he gave standing another try and succeeded. She glanced toward the back of the room, suddenly aware of the vulnerable position she'd put herself in. She didn't know "Al" from Adam, and the bulge in the front of his painted-on jeans suggested a more-than-casual interest in spending time with her. Tensing, she reached for her phone.

"I'm afraid you have the advantage on me, ma'am." He remained where he stood, not approaching her. Did he realize her concerns?

"What?" She grasped the device and brought it close to her, ready to speed-dial 911 if necessary.

"I gave you my name, but I don't know yours."

"Orlena...Orlena Estelle. I'm the schoolteacher here." She watched him, looking for the slightest sign of danger. Deep inside, her cougar sniffed the air and relaxed. Some comfort, but a woman alone in a 150-

year-old building with a strange man with a hard-on couldn't be too careful. Even if she was considering very naughty behavior.

"That's a mighty pretty name." He lapsed into the lingo they were encouraged to use while on the crowded street, but somehow, coming from him, it wasn't trite at all. "Since I am here with a little time— my cattle are penned for the night—maybe I might persuade you to allow me to buy you dinner? I know you schoolmarms don't drink."

If he only knew how good a drink sounded, but telling him would throw off the game. And she liked the game. So much. "Well, I have all these papers to grade." She batted her eyelashes at him then winced. Talk about trite.

He took a step toward her, and the temperature in the room went up ten degrees, the air thick, harder to breathe.

"Can they wait?"

She pressed back against the desk, his gaze holding her, trapping her like a butterfly on a pin. "Maybe, but"—she jumped back into the fantasy— "the school board doesn't like unmarried teachers being seen around town with strange men."

Two more steps, and he was so close she could smell a woodsy cologne, faint but present, and the scent of man, strong, enticing man. Her head spun. Al reached out, and she flinched. He stopped, giving her a moment, then took her hand in his and lifted it, palm up, to his lips. His stubble was sharp, and his lips were soft when he nuzzled her hand. Every nerve ending in her body went on full alert. Her cat purred.

"Far be it from me to endanger the purity of the town by seducing the schoolmarm." He dropped her hand and leaned in to lift an errant curl from beside her cheek. "But, darlin', you make a man forget himself."

She rubbed her fingers over his cheek and traced his mouth. Al caught her wrist and drew a fingertip into his mouth. His lips closed around it, and he softly touched it with the tip of his tongue and then bit down, just the edges of his teeth sliding along it as she withdrew. She shook hard with an arousal she hadn't even known was possible.

"I thank you for your consideration."

Bracing herself, she drew a breath, trying not to

pant. How could he have this effect on her? He was no cougar, nor any other shifter. Her cat would know. But a mere human shouldn't be able to generate the rumbling purr inside her head or the rush of moisture to her womanly parts.

"Perhaps some other time."

He rested a hand on her waist and tugged her closer until they melded from the hips down and the protrusion in his pants rubbed against her aching pussy. Through all the layers of her dress, petticoats, and pantalets, she shouldn't be able to feel a thing, but she did. Oh, she did.

He rocked his hips against her. "You wouldn't send me out onto the cold, empty range without even a kiss, would you?"

Cupping her chin, he tilted her head, and she let him. He brushed his lips against hers firmly—not intrusive but encouraging.

"It's so lonely out there," he murmured. "Just one kiss to remember when I'm all alone."

A small thing, and his heat, his scent, his strong arms tightening around her, holding her to him, dropped her square into the fantasy. When he took possession of her mouth, she had no strength to fight. Al's hands slid down under her bustle and lifted her to sit on the desk. He moved closer, nudging her legs apart with his own, exploring her mouth while she whimpered under his touch.

He trailed his hands up her sides, along the corset boning that held her upright and made it nearly impossible to bend or draw a deep breath. She'd hated it until he brought his mouth to her ear and praised it in warm breaths that tightened things deep inside her. "Mmm, such a womanly shape, tiny waist and bountiful breasts I'm dying to touch. Can I...may I just rub my thumb over your nipples like this, ma'am?"

A little late to ask when he already circled tightened peaks that had suddenly become so sensitive she arched her back, pressing them into his touch. He pinched one, and she shivered. He nuzzled down to where the stiff lace scratched her neck and loosed a button. Then another, following his fingers with his lips. She clutched his T-shirt at the waist for balance. Even sitting was too hard to manage without help when her bodice parted to reveal her chemise and the corset lifting her breasts like an offering to his eager touch.

"Oh, sweetheart, you are so beautiful. I have to have a taste."

She strangled on her breath as he laid her back on the big teacher's desk, knocking the little lamp to the floor where the lightbulb went out with a pop. She didn't care. Al tugged the chemise down, baring her breasts to the rising moonlight. He groaned and traced a fingertip around one of her nipples. She focused on getting air in and out of her lungs, but, when he bent his head and drew the aching tip into the warm cave of his mouth, she sobbed in pleasure and desire.

He licked, toying with her until she dug her hands into his hair—soft and without sticky product—and pulled. Lifting his gaze, he smiled around her breast and gave a deep suck, and bit down.

She shrieked.

Releasing her, he gave her that wicked smile again. "Miss Estelle, may I have the pleasure of fucking you?"

*Dear God.* She nodded and lay panting as he

tugged her to the edge of the desk and rolled her skirt up to her waist. Her pantalets were in the way, but he drew them down her legs, kissing each knee, and then knelt right there between them. "But, first, I want you to come in my mouth."

Orlena grabbed her skirts and held them flat, staring down the line of her body to see the dark head at the apex of her thighs. The garters holding up her stockings were a frilly addition to the most erotic scene in her life. No, it wasn't her first time out of the gate, but it was the first time she'd done it in such feminine clothes, and the first time with a man who seemed to know his way around a pussy.

He stroked her, gliding through the moisture of her arousal, and then flattened one hand on her belly and thrust two fingers on the other hand inside her, hooking them toward the front to meet the pressure of his palm on the outside. She climbed, rising higher and faster toward orgasm, but when he closed his mouth over her clit and sucked, she dropped over, shaking and shuddering and with a sensation like flying.

Al lifted his face, moisture slicking his lips. "You

make a man proud, Miss Estelle, and you taste so sweet."

Before she could come back to earth, he'd opened his pants and brought his cock—hard, long, and with a big, smooth head—to her cunt. She locked her stockinged legs around his waist, and he plunged in, nearly rending her..

Inside, he paused, allowing her to adjust to his girth. It had been so long, and he was so big.... Could he fit all the way in?

"Shhh, you're fine, fine." He glided back a bit then all the way in again. "You just need to come some more."

*Again?* She could barely think. But he pressed a thumb to her clit and circled in time with his thrusts into her body, in and out, deeper, until he stretched her wide enough to take all of him, then out and in again. For so long, he rode her, and, with each drive, he rubbed over the sweet spot she hadn't believed in until now. She flew high and far again, higher, falling off a cliff into an abyss with no bottom as he shot his cum into her, searing her and marking her forever.

He fell over her on the desk, bracing himself on his

forearms and panting. The moon rose to fill the window, almost full—it would be full in twenty-four hours. She ran a hand over his chest and contemplated the amazing surprise the evening had brought. Tomorrow would be so busy with the crowds in town to see the ghostly antics the lunar cycle brought.

*The moon!*

Dear God, what had she done?

She'd done more than have a quickie with a tourist lost in a fantasy. Tomorrow, when the full moon rose, "Al" might be undergoing some major changes he hadn't anticipated. And the pride was going to have her head.

The first rule a young female in the pride learned was to never have unprotected sex with an ordinary human on the night of the full moon—or within twenty four hours of it—unless it was with the express intent of creating another shifter. The mingling of souls inherent in such a connection when the veils were already thin made it possible for a cat spirit to enter the person. It didn't happen every time, and none of the elders seemed to know why it was so hit and miss, but it was a foolish chance to take.

And she'd taken it without thought, with a complete stranger.

Not good, not good at all.

# Chapter Three

Somewhere far from her fantasy, a door banged closed. Orlena's foggy mind cleared in an instant. If anyone found them here, she would never hear the end of it. Perhaps nothing had happened—perhaps he wouldn't change, and nobody needed to know at all.

But if Tex found them, no explanation would suffice.

"You've got to get out of here!" In a careless moment, Orlena had broken every rule governing her life. She had given away something not hers to share. Rather, it was, but she'd not planned to pass it along to someone who would have no idea what to do with it.

What would happen if he did change the next

night? She knew nothing about him. She had allowed loneliness and a trip to a past she'd spent so much time in recently to cloud her reality. She was not a schoolmarm in 1870 but a middle-school teacher in 2015. Her curriculum was not reading, writing, and 'rithmetic, but social studies, citizenship, and computer skills.

Al still lay over her, breathing heavily.

She shoved at him. "I mean it, off me!"

Panic replaced the golden moment of closeness with another person. It would have been nice to blame it on her cougar, especially since its purr had not stopped since she'd come close to the handsome stranger, but it had been her decision.

Why would the cat be interested in someone not of their ilk? Crazy kitty had steered her right into disaster.

Finally her "rancher" lover pushed himself to his feet and freed her to leap to hers—except she couldn't. Her knees trembled as she tried to stand up, and her heart thudded in her throat.

To her surprise, after their lovemaking, he was even more attractive than before. The moonlight cast magic on everything in the room, and she wondered if he'd be as gorgeous a cat as a man. Would he have thick fur? Would it be light or dark? The eyes stayed the same color when they shifted...so he'd have distinctive indigo eyes. She shivered. The light and shadows on his face gave him a godlike mien. Her cat yowled, and she gave it a mental shush.

Whatever had happened, she would have to keep an eye on him and see what happened the following night when the lunar orb reached its full power. The very least she could do was damage control.

How would he feel if he had to move to town?

The alpha and elders would never allow a new cat to leave until they could see how he reacted to the change. Some new ones went quite insane.

Or maybe nothing would happen.

But from nightfall tomorrow on, she couldn't let him out of her sight. It would probably be better to keep him close until then, if possible.

He extended a hand to her. "If we're in a hurry, you might want to stand up."

*Hurry?* She shook her head, refocusing on the moment. Orlena ignored his helpful gesture and pushed her mussed hair from her face. "Thanks, I'm good." She listened hard but heard no footsteps, nothing to indicate anyone had entered the building. "Did you close the door behind you when you came in?"

With the front door dead-bolted, he had to have come in the basement entrance after her; it had a tendency to stick, and she didn't remember if she'd checked.

He paused in zipping up his pants. "I think it closed automatically behind me, why?"

"Nothing." Perhaps it had been the wind, or maybe even her guilty imagination. But Tex's uncanny ability to show up where she least wanted him was not to be dismissed. "If you're ready, let's go."

She grabbed her small handbag, an antique that matched her dress, marched to the door, and waited while he tucked in the body-hugging T-shirt that made her wonder why she'd never been into the sexiness of men's arms. The muscles in Al's could have their own hunk calendar.

Arriving at her side, he wrapped one of those arms

around her and pulled her to him. "You're in an awful hurry to be rid of me."

Orlena stiffened, but his body heat—a little too warm—melted her into his tall frame, and she tilted her head back in anticipation of another of his drugging kisses. He complied, brushing his lips over hers then urging them open and mingling his breath with hers. Sweet, she half-noticed. He'd probably been sipping one of those spicy sarsaparillas the saloon sold so many of, and she could taste herself, something that shouldn't be turning her on so soon. After a long, indulgent while, they broke apart.

His cock, ready again for action, ground into her belly.

"I'm not." She nuzzled his cheek, like a cat scenting something it liked a lot. "Really."

He blinked down at her with heavy-lidded eyes. "Not...what?"

She laughed. "Not trying to be rid of you." *Not by a long shot.* In fact, she couldn't leave him until morning, to be safe, and then had to be at his side again before the sun sank. "I was going to invite you for something to eat." *And then make sure I keep you there all night long.* "Have you had dinner?"

He turned her away from him and gave her a pat on her twisted bustle. Darn it. If she couldn't bend the wire cage back into shape, she'd have to get another one.

"Nope, but I'd be delighted to take you out for a bite. What's good in town?"

"If you don't mind pot luck, we can go to my place." She offered what she hoped was an innocent smile, but his eyes narrowed.

"You're up to something, but I can't quite figure it out."

"Shhh, come on." She locked the classroom and headed down the hall toward the front stairs, feeling in her purse for the key to the big double doors. If someone was heading up the back way, she'd rather risk being seen on the main street than encounter Tex—which was probably why her cat had stopped purring and was emitting a low growl. Kitty didn't want him in her life any more than her human side did.

She was due at the saloon for final preparations for the following night in an hour but wanted to get

Al out of town long before that. She'd think of an excuse to text as soon as she reached home.

Surefooted, another benefit of her ilk, she led the way down the wide front stairs and unlocked the door. Peering left and right, she was relieved to see the streets nearly deserted and the only a few tourists in sight. She grasped Al's hand and tugged him down the side street opposite the one he'd entered by, to where her car was parked. When she twisted the passenger-side lock on her Land Cruiser—the automatic anything long gone dead—he rested his hand on hers.

"Orlena, why don't we take my car?"

Because if my car is here then Tex will know I left with someone, and he will probably come snooping around to see who. "I live off-road a bit, up a dirt track." Another truth, at least. "Do you have four-wheel drive?"

To her relief, he shook his head and slid into the passenger seat.

"No, and I'd rather not take a rental up a dirt track anyway. Pretty sure the company wouldn't like it all scratched up."

She scooted around the car, exhaling with relief, and reached under her skirt to tighten the tapes on the bustle, narrowing it so she could fit behind the wheel. Rather than driving up to Main Street, she made a U-turn and drove down a block to the smaller street to parallel it for a few blocks. If her instincts were at all correct, by now Tex had followed them outside, and she did not need him to figure out she had a man with her. He didn't have a key to her classroom, so his ability to scent what they'd been up to would be limited.

As they joined the highway north of town, picking up speed, she rolled her window down and allowed the desert breeze to ruffle her hair. The scents of sage and wood smoke from someone's stove relaxed her. "We'll be there in a few minutes. It's not far."

Pushing a button, she turned on the radio and the swingy strains of some ancient country-western tune filled the car, making conversation unnecessary. She hoped. Her passenger seemed content to ride, for the moment, and she slowed at the dirt track she'd mentioned and made a left.

"Hang on, it gets bumpy." Washboard, actually,

for a few moments, and she suppressed a smile when Al clutched at the "oh, shit" strap as the tires struggled to grip the slippery surface.

But she was used to the rough road and loved the privacy living in her great-granddaddy's abandoned mining cabin afforded her. It also made her weekend mining efforts easier. After steering almost straight toward the foothills, she made a sharp left off the narrow track and onto one just wide enough for the vehicle.

The radio station faded into static, and he clicked it off. "You weren't kidding about being a bumpy road. How much farther? My teeth are aching from clacking together."

"About a half-mile or so." She cast him a sideways grin. "Bet your rent-a-car would have been pretty beat up by now, huh?"

"At least."

They emerged from the canyon and climbed the switchback road up the mountain face.

She let up on the gas. "Look down."

He leaned toward her and peered out her window. "Whoa."

"Yep. Pretty, isn't it?" The valley floor lay far below, the sparse flickering lights of Goldland in the near distance, the brighter ones of the big town farther out. "Once we were bigger than Tonopah is now, much bigger." She leaned past him to point. "See that dark spot between two buildings in our town? That is my grandmother's home. I own it, but unless I can save enough money to shore it up, it will be a heap of lumber within a few years."

"So that's why you live in the back of beyond," he replied in a quiet, thoughtful voice.

She laughed, a harsh bark of bitterness she couldn't always suppress. "Partly. I do love it up here, and I mine on the weekends." She straightened and drove on up the bumpy dirt road, steering around blind corners with the ease of long practice. "But it would be convenient to be able to stay in town during the school week."

"What do you do in winter?" He half hung out his window, where the twisting road had again placed the view, and she rolled her eyes. He was already hypnotized by her mountains. "Doesn't it get pretty snowy up here?"

"If it's bad, I stay with a teacher friend in town, but I also have a Snowcat. I just park at the highway and zoom on in."

Around one more bend, the reason Orlena loved her home became clear, as she'd promised. A small, almost shack-like board house perched a couple of feet above where the road ended. She stopped and hopped out of the Land Cruiser, and Alden followed, agape at the natural beauty surrounding them. As she strode up the path toward her weathered house, the thunder of a waterfall somewhere on the opposite canyon wall drowned out even the wind.

The scrub of the lower altitudes had been magically replaced by stately pines and quivering aspens, scenting the air with their resins and lending a sense of peace unlike any he'd ever experienced. Even if the building itself was old and had a sagging porch, the setting more than made up for it. And directly ahead of him, Orlena's bustled bottom was even more stunning than the heavens above with their star fields and comets.

As they arrived at the steps, the luminous orb of

the moon topped the mountains and seemed to beam right down on the roof of the ancient building. Not tin, as he'd first supposed, but a more modern sort of dark-colored metal roof. At least one improvement had been made in the last hundred-plus years. Orlena paused on the top step, and he gripped the handrail to avoid bumping into her, the smooth wood under his palm either new or made splinter-free from the passage of time. He believed the former.

"Hang on a second and let me light a lantern." She ducked inside and rattled around for moment before a light flickered inside. "Okay, come in. I didn't want you to trip over anything."

He entered and paused to get a feel for the interior while Orlena lit a couple more lanterns and a brace of candles on the stone mantelpiece. "No electricity up here?"

She waved toward a kitchenette on one side of the room. "Yes, but my generator is mostly for the refrigerator and a couple of other essentials—like my laptop."

Made sense, even if he didn't think he could live without all his electronics. "Internet?"

"Satellite, yes."

"TV?" Had she ever seen *Not on My Watch*? She certainly didn't seem to recognize him. Perhaps his worry about giving his full name had been for nothing. He hated being called Al.

She wrinkled her nose. "Sorry, no. There's nothing I like enough to waste the time or the electricity on. Besides, I have one at school, if I do care to catch anything." She opened a door, and he could see a bed piled with quilts and fluffy pillows. "I'm going to change into something more comfortable."

She slipped inside but didn't close the door, just stepped out of view and rattled some drawers, opened and closed something.

His cock twitched at the thought of what she might be changing into. Maybe a lacy nightgown like a schoolmarm might have worn. He could get into that. Yes, he could.

"Why?" she called from somewhere in the bedroom. "Do you watch a lot of TV? Do you have nothing better to do with your free time?

He chuckled, trying not to be too offended at her disdain for his livelihood. "No reality shows for you, then? Game shows? Sitcoms?" He drew a breath. "Ghost-chasing shows?"

Orlena's head appeared in the doorway, brow furrowed. "What? No."

She disappeared, and he wondered at her vehemence. The debunker in him surfaced, and, while the lecher in him pondered whether she was naked and if she would reappear in something sexy, Alden Strong, protector of the public from fakery and fraud, remembered his mission.

He was supposed to be in town, strolling the streets, watching for preparations for the full moon when most of the ghostly activity would occur. Buying people drinks to get them to spill their guts. Tomorrow, thousands of people would clog the streets, shopping at the stores, eating at the restaurants, buying souvenirs, and waiting for the sun to set.

They were expecting a big show. And Alden was planning to waylay that show, to expose the tricks and strings, hidden wires, and flashing "orbs" created by some guy at a control board. Reveal how they created the full-body apparition known as the Indigo

Princess.

He had only tonight to find it all.

Instead, he had followed this pretty girl into the back of nowhere for a bite to eat and maybe another chance at seeing her naked.

What was wrong with him? No woman had managed to distract him from his important work before.

Maybe it wasn't ghostliness, but witchery, that the people of Goldland had to share.

Alden strode across the main room toward the single window. He skirted a sofa and dining table, both probably almost as old as the shack itself. Someone—Orlena?—had put their money into the new roof rather than spending it on furnishings. Practical. Her teacher's salary in the impoverished town probably didn't stretch far. Her vehicle was a late 1980s vintage, best he could guess, and her Snowcat might not be much newer.

The moonlit landscape beckoned, trees mounting the slope behind. If he wasn't in such a hurry to return to his work, he'd suggest a hike up there. How long since he'd been out on a mountain trail with a pretty girl? College?

He'd been too busy since then, leveraging his journalism degree into a local weekend anchor desk then moving up the food chain until he landed a national slot. The watchdog angle.... That had come by accident, when he'd uncovered a plot to steal seniors' savings and the network had liked it. But lately, he spent more time disproving the paranormal than the financial. The network liked that, too. Spooky happenings drew bigger ratings than keeping old people from starving, sadly.

"Okay, back."

He turned to see Orlena's idea of more comfortable. Long, dark hair brushed out and pulled back in a high ponytail. Jeans, a T-shirt, and...hiking boots? She carried a daypack over to the kitchen area. "We going somewhere?"

"Up the mountain a ways. I wanted to show you something special."

"I thought we were going to eat here and then you could take me back to my hotel." Not that he wanted to go, but duty called.

"Oh...well, it's only about a half hour up. I thought

I'd stuff some cheese and crackers and fruit, a bottle of wine, in here, and we could have a picnic."

"At night?" How bad was a half-hour, but in the wilds? "Aren't there bears or mountain lions or something?"

She faced away from him, so he couldn't see her expression, but she froze, her shoulders stiff. "Probably not. I go up there all the time. It's near the old silver mine where I work on the weekends."

"Isn't mining pretty dangerous to do on your own?"

Or did she have help...some burly miner type who hoped to catch the pretty lady's attention? He bristled at the thought.

"It helps pay the bills, and I like the solitude." She zipped the pack and turned around. "But if you don't want to go, if you're scared of the wildlife, we can eat here."

He shrugged. "Well, I did come to soak up some of the scary nighttime stuff in town. But I can spare the time."

She slung the pack over her shoulder. "Sure, it won't take long. Come on, it's an easy climb, and you won't regret it." Nearing him, Orlena brushed her lips across his ear, warm breath melting his knees. "I promise."

Visions of this newly modern version of his sexy schoolmarm naked in the moonlight tore away any thoughts of immediate return. "If you don't think I'll miss any full-body apparitions in the saloon or clanking chains in the drugstore?"

"You won't. It should be pretty quiet tonight."

Confidence colored her tones and brought his suspicions about her involvement in the scam back to life, but, as she headed for the door, the pack slung over her shoulders, her fanny in tight jeans drew his attention, and he followed. Usually a leader, he'd never spent so much time behind a woman in his life. In her case, the view was worth it.

"You aren't trying to keep me out of town, are you? Holding me hostage?"

She tossed a grin at him over her shoulder. "Would you mind if I was?"

# Chapter Four

Orlena led Al up the narrow trail on her mission of distraction. She'd considered cooking something easy and eating in the shack, but she wanted activities guaranteed to take time and keep him with her as long as possible. As in, overnight. She'd return him to town the next morning when she went, as late as possible. Tex would bitch her out for her absence, but the text she'd sent while in the bedroom had indicated vague female trouble, and he wouldn't press for details. Males were all alike that way, cats, people...wolves, from what she'd heard. And she'd shut her phone down after that to avoid any annoying discussion.

Her people were her first concern, and, though the ghost of the Indigo Princess provided an income for them, she wasn't that thrilled about deceiving people. Even less about the extent of her involvement. For the next twenty-four hours, she would have to keep an eye on her tourist and make sure he didn't transform into a big cat. If he did...there would be no hiding her mistake.

If not, she could slip away from him and leave him to his devices. He'd go back to wherever he came from, and she'd have one hell of a memory.

As promised, the trail was not bad—by her standards. Behind her, she heard a little huffing and puffing and the scrape of a shoe on the loose scree. Pausing, she waited for him to catch up. A light breeze rattled the aspen leaves, but the waterfall's roar and crash this close nearly drowned them out.

"You okay?"

He arrived at her side, his jaunty hair stuck to his face with perspiration. "Sure." He bent forward, hands on his knees, and panted. "I do this every day."

Sure he did. Orlena found advantage to the proceedings. By the time she was done with him and they returned to the shack, he'd be too tired to want to go anywhere that night. She'd make it her business to ensure that outcome. Even if she had to spend the whole night in his arms. No sacrifice was too great for her people.

Now to get him naked.

And hard.

"We are almost there, just around the next bend."

He kept looking off into the distance, where shadows blended with stray moonlight under the dark pines. "You sure there aren't any bears or wildcats around here?"

There had better not be any other cats around.

"Not at the moment," she answered truthfully. Her own would have let her know if there were danger, especially from cougars. This was her range. No strays were welcome. And even pride members had to get permission to enter, as she would have to for their territory. "We're fine. Don't you want to see the surprise?"

"In a minute." He was still out of breath. Perhaps she'd underestimated the effect of the altitude on a flatlander.

Actually...she knew nothing about him. He knew more about her—unusual for a member of a secretive pride like hers.

She planted her butt on a rock, unwilling to stand while he got his act together. Would his cat have trouble adjusting? Everyone she knew was either from Goldland or another mountainous area. *Ugh.* With any luck, he wouldn't even have a cat and would just enjoy the entertainment tomorrow and then go on his way. Although, he was kind of cute and certainly energetic in the sex department, she wasn't in the mate market. A man like this would be nothing less than an alpha if he shifted, and fending off one alpha was all she cared to deal with.

But she didn't know anything about him. Maybe she should. Orlena patted the rock next to her. "Plenty of room for two. Join me?"

Al dropped next to her with a sigh and accepted a bottle of water from the pack. "Best offer I've had all day."

He tipped the water back, and his throat moved as he swallowed. Who knew an Adam's apple could be so sexy?

She pretend-pouted. "Best offer? Really?"

He chuckled then coughed. "Well, almost. But this

one may save my life."

Orlena punched his shoulder. "It's not that bad, is it?"

Al sucked in air through his nose and let it out in a long stream. "No, not while I'm sitting. But if it's much farther, I may have to cry off. It's getting pretty late. And I'm apparently out of shape."

"Where are you from, anyway?"

He looked away from her. "Far away from here. I travel a lot."

"But, originally?"

"California, San Diego."

He wasn't giving her much information, and she didn't want to do anything to push him away. It would be much easier if he wanted to stick around for the night than if he became annoyed. Men didn't like pushy women, or so she'd heard. At least he wasn't making up a long story full of lies like her *big mistake* in college had.

She jumped to her feet; she'd have to ask her questions at the falls, maybe while they ate. After. Men were pretty pliable in the afterglow, weren't they? She had no idea. With her limited bedpost notches, she didn't have a lot to compare it to. But she couldn't let him head downhill. Grabbing his hand, she urged him upright. "If you need to get back early, we'd better head on up there. Time's a-wasting."

He linked his fingers with hers and kissed her cheek. "I wish I didn't have to."

*What? A chink in his secretive armor?* "Why do you need to? There won't be any activity tonight, you know."

He pulled her closer, one brow arched high. "How can you be so sure?"

*Because the ghost is out of town.* But the truth wouldn't do. She couldn't share their secrets with a stranger. Even if he might be one of them by accident in the near future. "Well, there might be some minor hauntings, but that's it. Because the full moon isn't until tomorrow, even if it is gorgeous tonight. The Indigo Princess appears only one night a month."

The brow lowered—about halfway. "I see. For a minute, I thought you might know the spirits personally." They walked side by side, hands still linked. "Do you believe in ghosts?"

His casual question pricked at her guilt, and, with relief, she rounded the bend and waved to the tumbling falls and pool below her. "I believe in the extraordinary. In things most people never see."

"Is that steam?"

*Distraction successful.*

It was a start.

"Yes." Orlena pulled her hand free and shrugged her pack from her shoulders. "Mind if we swim before we eat?"

He leaned so far over, ogling the plummeting water, she grabbed the back of his shirt, fearing he might fall. It wasn't too far, but she didn't want him hitting his head.

"Okay, let's have a swim." She dragged a couple of towels out of the pack and hung their dinner on a branch over the pool. "Just in case one of those bears you mentioned shows up."

His expression made her laugh and feel a little guilty. She'd know long before any large animal arrived to steal their goodies, but it would also keep it off the ground and out of the reach of ants and other insects for a while.

"I didn't bring anything to swim in," he warned.

"Me either." Orlena lifted her shirt over her head and faced away from him. "A little help?"

Any hesitation he'd had was not obvious in the strong arms that tugged her to him and wrapped around her body, cupping her breasts through her bra. "Swimming is sounding better all the time, if it means you're going to be naked."

"The hooks are in the back."

He chuckled and bent to nip at her neck. "I'll get to them. But you smell so good, and you're so warm."

Yes, her body temp was a couple degrees warmer than the average person's, but she couldn't get into that. He might have to know the truth soon enough. "It's the cool breeze. Makes me seem like that where my clothes covered me." She shivered, although it wasn't especially cold. "Let's get in the water, and we'll both be warm. Hooks, please."

But he seemed in no hurry to release her, just squeezed her tighter to him, palming her boobs.

"I kind of hate to let go of you." The hard ridge of his cock dug into her ass cheeks, the fabric of the two pairs of jeans between their skin almost no obstacle.

"But I would like to see you naked."

In one move he pushed her away and freed her tits from their cotton-and-wire prison.

"No problem, if we're both going to be that way." The things she would do for her pride. Orlena bent to untie her boots, and Al grabbed her hips and dragged her close again. "I thought you wanted me naked," she said, her voice muffled from being bent in two. "We aren't going to get anywhere like this."

He ground his cock against her, and she stifled a moan.

"No, but I do like the position you're in." Releasing her, he stepped back, and she managed to get rid of the rest of her clothes before he went after her again.

"Noted," she said. "See you in the water."

Orlena raced forward and launched into a perfect dive over the pool twenty or more feet below. Heart in his throat, Alden ran after her and peered over the steep drop to see her naked body slice through the waterfall and land with a splash.

Through the steam, he could see her waving to him, and he considered the options. Dive and take a chance on death or paralysis? He'd been on the diving team in high school, the year his parochial school made nationals in fact, but safety dictated not going headfirst anywhere he'd not ensured was deep enough to avoid injury.

Still, Orlena had done it. If he aimed for the falls, he should be all right...right?

Or wuss out and scramble down the slope to meet her? It looked like more loose scree, and the likelihood of injury was probably greater there. He wore sneakers, decent for the average trail, but without the grip of a hiking boot.

"Come on," she called, swimming aside and pointing to the falls. "The water's fine."

He stripped to the skin, kicking his shoes off and whispering a prayer to.... Which saint covered idiocy? Catholic school was long behind him, so he went with St. Anthony, the saint in charge of lost things, who never failed to help him find his keys. He might help him recover his sanity—at least his focus.

Straight-bodied, arms outstretched, he fell forward as he had in Acapulco when a dare during a night of too-much tequila led to a morning of cliff-diving. It couldn't be any harder. The cool air parted before him as he plummeted into the steam rising from the waterfall. He aimed for the same spot she'd hit and sank into the extraordinary sensation of gliding through hot spray into the warm depths of a pool that went down at least twenty feet.

Surfacing, Alden broke into a laugh and looked around for Orlena. She swam to his side, a grin creasing her face.

"You actually did it." She rested her hands on his shoulders and kicked her feet slowly, treading water. "And like a pro."

"Well, *you* did it." He withheld his diving medals for another time. After all, he hadn't made the Olympic team. Quite. "What a blast. I've never seen anything like this. The falls are hot."

She nodded. "The source is right above them, a volcanic hot springs in a cave near the mine. You'd never be able to handle the temperature there. It would cook the flesh from your bones. The air cools the water before it hits the pool."

Invigorated, he made a mental note to do a little diving in his spare time. He'd missed the experience, having reduced his workouts to just what the studio gym could provide in stolen moments. What other parts of life had he set aside in pursuing his career?

Orlena slid her palms from his shoulders and circled his neck. When her lips met his, he knew the answer to his question. A busy man had no time for relationships, barely time for meaningless sex, which he'd set aside a while back when he realized it left him lonely afterward. Most men seemed fine with it, but as he stroked wet hair from her face and parted her lips with his tongue, he remembered why it was bad and lovemaking was good.

Not that he was in love with Orlena. Or she with him. But he couldn't deny something magical— haunting—about her touched him in a place where lusty fans and sexy co-workers didn't. He kicked his legs, moving them both until his feet reached a sandy bottom and he could get leverage. With her thighs wrapped around his waist, her breasts bobbed on the surface of the water. He dug his fingers into her ass cheeks and sank to the hilt inside warm, slick woman.

Neither Saint Anthony nor anyone else was going to be able to save his sanity this time.

He might never get another opportunity to spend a night with her—and he could do his research in the morning. She clenched around him and dropped her mouth to suck on the side of his neck.

He'd have a hickey.

She'd marked him.

He would do the same, given half a chance. Maybe a little lower though.

Her skin under his palms was warm silk, slippery in the water, but he tightened his grip and lifted and lowered her, savoring the tight fist of her pussy. How long since he'd felt a connection like this with a woman? Never. She rippled around him, and he nipped her shoulder, relishing her moans. She was so responsive he longed to spend a week in her bed, buried balls-deep in her pussy, her mouth, her ass, if she'd let him. He lapped at a droplet of water on her breast and sucked her nipple into his mouth.

She gasped something, a strangled cry, and convulsed around his cock. He thrust a few more times and followed her into mind-bending pleasure, legs buckling under him as he shot his cum inside her hot sheath.

As they both went under the water and emerged spluttering, he realized that for the first—Dear God, second tonight!—time in his adult life, he'd fucked a woman bareback. The repercussions could be enormous.

# Chapter Five

The sun rose over the mountains before either of them left her bed back at the cabin.

Orlena stretched and admired how a shaft of sunlight caught the streaks of lighter brown, almost gold, in Al's hair. Even after a trip through the waterfall, swim in the pool, a quick shower, and two more sessions of lovemaking during the night—with condoms from his wallet—her visitor still looked like a model from some stylist's magazine. She reached out to touch the lock falling over his forehead, but her attention drifted to the sheet pulled up just below his waist, and she took the opportunity to catalogue his good points.

Broad shoulders, a sprinkling of hair on his firm,

muscled chest, flat, toned abs, and a narrow happy trail leading down under the sheet to the playground she'd enjoyed so thoroughly the night before. What a shame after tonight he'd be on his way back to....

Well, she'd never even gotten around to asking him what he did for a living. He'd told her where he was originally from but not where he lived now.

If he was married.

The question seemed more relevant than it would have before, although she forced herself not to think beyond today. But if she'd created another cougar, albeit by mistake, perhaps he might stay. A rumble from deep inside was more cougar than hunger.

What was she thinking? Even if he was single and had the urge to set up shop in a dilapidated ghost town with an income entirely based on defrauding tourists...she hadn't known him a full twenty-four hours. Her cat rolled and purred, delighted to be next to him. Did she know something the human didn't?

Nothing in the lore indicated that doing it twice made it more likely to create a shifter. It seemed as if they either "took" or didn't. But still, taking a chance like that....

Living alone with no sex life for a long time could make a girl do ridiculous things. She'd call it lust and try not to consider how much she liked having him there with her.

Shrug it off and enjoy the morning, at least.

With a hint of mischief, she lifted the covers and reached underneath to find him already halfway erect. It would be a shame to waste it. Orlena ducked under the sheet and fisted his cock, squeezing and noting with pleasure the instant reaction. Like satin-covered steel, and she hadn't even had him in her mouth yet. He'd been too busy fucking her silly.

But she was in no mood to let him leave without savoring the taste of him. She wanted the whole experience.

Stretching her jaw wide, she took him in, stroking the head with her tongue as she did. A deep groan emerged from outside her hiding place, and she smiled around him.

"Baby, your mouth is so hot, it's almost burning me."

She tried to lift her head, but his hands clamped on it, holding her in place.

"No, don't stop." He rocked his hips, and she grazed him with her teeth. He jerked and groaned. Gliding up and down his length, she eased him deeper. As he went rigid, she took his balls in her hand and gave a squeeze. With a roar any shifter would be proud of, he poured his cum down her throat, trembling head to foot.

Orlena swallowed every drop and wiped her mouth on the sheet before emerging to smile at him.

"Breakfast?"

He lay panting. "I need a nap first."

Orlena sighed. "But you just woke up."

"Sweetheart, I slept half an hour all night. With that sweet pussy mine for the taking, I didn't want to waste the time." He pulled a pillow over his face and was snoring gently in a moment.

Too edgy to lie there any longer, she slipped out of bed and padded naked for the door. Out of sight of the house, she shifted—bones cracking, vision enhancing, hearing sharpening. She usually let her kitty hunt every night, but she'd been occupied. It was time to let the cat run.

Racing up the same trail, savoring the muscles

that lengthened to allow her to cover vast stretches without tiring, she passed the falls in a quarter of the time they had the night before. Farther along, she passed the tree line and ran on open ground. The early sun caressed her fur; scents of small animals scurrying for cover delighted her nose. Claws gripped in a surefooted way she could never accomplish otherwise.

They'd scrambled to the top of the hill above the pool, laughing, the night before, awkward on two legs. Now, she had no such issues. She looped the fringes of her territory and finally found the spot where another cat had crossed the boundaries. A strong, musky male scent and a claw mark on a tree. Tex hadn't tried to hide his presence—he'd wanted her to know he'd been there.

But he hadn't approached the house. She'd have known.

He'd invaded only far enough to make a statement. One she intended to strike down right after breakfast. No cat, alpha or otherwise, was welcome on her range without invitation. With her own cougar as upset as she was, she gave up on the joy of a run and loped downhill toward the shack. It might be her last chance to spend a few moments alone with the first man she'd been with in years.

And she wasn't going to waste it.

Shifting back, she ran down the last few yards to the house and inside, where she started a pot of coffee and slid some bacon into a skillet to fry. The little animals had been safe. She hadn't hunted, and she was starving.

She dug out another pan, cracked eggs in, and stirred.

"Can I help?"

Orlena drew a breath, inhaling the scent of clean male. "You showered."

He stood close behind her, resting his palms on her hips. "And you cook naked."

She hadn't given it a thought. Hunger and the habit of living alone had driven her lack of clothing straight from her mind. Still....

"Only when I have special guests. Do you like sourdough pancakes?"

He nuzzled the nape of her neck, sending molten heat to the swollen lips between her thighs. "I'm not sure I've had them." His hands explored upward, cupping her breasts and molding them, grinding his jeans-clad groin against her bare ass. "But I am very hungry."

"I guess cheese and crackers aren't enough to hold a man who's been so busy all night." Or a woman who'd not only enjoyed strenuous lovemaking but a cat shift to raise her appetite.

"I guess not." He nipped her, possessive and sharp, and she jumped. "Now, step aside and let me help you. You promised me pancakes."

Self-conscious all of a sudden, she moved into the bedroom and pulled on a robe, but in a few moments, she returned to assemble the ingredients and had three round, saucer-sized cakes bubbling on the griddle. Al finished the scrambled eggs and put the skillet on a trivet on the table, set the bacon to drain on paper toweling, and watched her with hungry eyes. Between them, she wagered they could eat all she'd made and more.

"I'm not a big breakfast eater, but wow." Alden dabbed at his mouth and blew out a breath. He, in fact, wasn't any kind of breakfast eater, but he'd demolished three eggs, half a dozen of the big hotcakes, and more strips of crispy bacon than he cared to count.

Orlena stacked their plates and took them to the sink. "Must be the mountain air."

"Or the cook." He gathered silverware and followed her. "I still don't see why you had to get dressed. You looked great."

"I had to get you to stop groping me, or we'd have burned the bacon...then where would we be?" She flashed him a shy grin, but her eyes held a mischievous sparkle.

"Back in bed?"

"Hungry." Filling a dishpan with soapy water, she put in all but the pots and pans. "And I hate to say it, but we need to get going shortly. I have a meeting at ten."

"It's Saturday," he reminded her. "You don't have school, right?"

She busied herself, wiping down the stove. "Town council." Tossing the sponge in the sink, she headed for the bathroom. "Give me ten minutes to shower and get ready."

He started for the sink, but she called back to him.

"Leave them. I'll get them tonight when I get home."

When *she* returned. Not when *they* did. She had no intention of bringing him back again, nor should she. After filming tonight, he'd be anathema, lucky not to be ridden out on a rail.

She'd hate him. Probably.

Was there any way to avoid it? He had no reason to think Orlena was involved in the whole haunting scam. Poor girl was likely just glad to see things getting better, the stores open longer hours, her town thriving for the first time in a long time.

She'd be just as horrified as his viewers when he unmasked the Indigo Princess. Perhaps even upset enough to leave with him?

He didn't have the slightest idea what her connections in Goldland were. Family? Friends? Orlena had hustled him out of town via a back street as if ashamed to be seen in public with him. She hadn't flicked an eyelash when he introduced himself and had expressed disdain for television. Surely that wasn't a ruse to throw him off the track.

Did she intend to keep him out of town until after the full moon? No...she'd indicated that they would be leaving in just a few minutes.

Orlena re-entered the living room in a chemise and some kind of slip. She held a corset to her abdomen and turned to face away from him. "Usually I wait until I'm in town to get in costume, but if you'll help, I can save the hassle. I hate having to haul all this gear into a small bathroom."

"Sure." He regarded the hanging strings with dismay. "What do I do?"

"Pull them as tight as you can. If I'm going to get into the dress I'm wearing today, I need a waist twenty-two inches or less."

He set to work, tugging the ribbons through the little holes, getting the two sides of the stiffened fabric as close together as possible. "Isn't that really small for a waist?"

She clutched the back of a chair, laughing, until he gave a jerk and her breath whooshed out of her lungs. "That's the way. Actually, no. In the silver boom of the 1870s, women wanted their waists a few inches smaller than that. But I'm a corset wuss. Fond of inhaling."

Fingers busy, he tried to keep his eyes on his task. If he let the ribbons drop, his hands would follow, and, once he got them on that rounded ass of hers, her petticoat would be over her head and she'd be bent over the table with his cock so deep he'd...she'd....

"Almost done back there?"

He swallowed hard and tied off the ends of the strings. "Yep, I think so." Unable to resist, he gave her a swat on her cotton-covered rump. "I wish we had time for a quickie."

She scooted away and giggled. "You're insatiable." Orlena disappeared into the bedroom but poked her head back out. "How long are you in town for, anyway?"

"Just until tomorrow, I think." Regret followed the words. He had never met anyone like Orlena. He wanted to ask her to get together that evening, but he'd be busy debunking the single thing her town had going for it. Then she'd either hail him as a hero for his great gift of truth or, more likely, hate him for it.

"Are you free for lunch? You've fed me twice. I owe you."

"I think I can get away for a bite." She emerged in a new dress, a heavy green fabric, also tight across the breasts and gathered back over that mouth-watering, taped-down-for-the-ride bustle. "As you probably guessed, I am a volunteer, playing the part of the 1870s schoolmarm you encountered yesterday. So, I will spend today wandering through town, speaking with children and adults alike about the schools once upon a time."

"You won't be in the school itself?"

"I'll be there some of the time." Orlena arched a brow and moved in front of a mirror hung on one weathered wall. She braided her hair and coiled it at her nape. "Dora will probably grab me and redo this, but it's authentic enough." She buttoned the last few tiny buttons at her throat and stuck a finger between the stiff collar and her neck. "I am glad I live in the twenty-first century and only have to dress like this a few days a month."

He trailed her out the door, hungry to know more about her. Once they reached town, he would have to make up for lost time, interview people who had been around the night before, and decide where to start filming once the sun went down. The crew was due around 2:00 p.m. After lunchtime.

"So, Dora...a friend?"

He couldn't imagine how she could slide so easily into the driver's seat with her stiff undergarments, but it did help explain her excellent posture. Although, no matter what she wore, anything or nothing, her movements embodied grace. Unlike the night before, he didn't take in the views of the mountains and high desert below. If he had no more time with her than this morning, he wanted to absorb everything about her. And lunch—they would eat together, but probably not alone. He'd rather have cheese and crackers above a waterfall in the moonlight with Schoolmarm Orlena than the finest meal in the nicest restaurant with anyone else.

Unsettling thought.

"She's another teacher, a very good friend."

*Who?* Oh, right, he'd asked about Dora. She'd mentioned other relatives by virtue of her dilapidated home in town and the mine shack...but none living.

"Any family hereabouts?" *Or a boyfriend?*

She steered down the steep track with easy skill. "My brother, but he's away right now. On business. And, of course, my sister-in-law and the kids. They are visiting her mother, or I would love to introduce you."

"Seems like a nice place to raise a family." And a pretty woman like her would probably want one. Especially a teacher. She must love children to do that job.

"Rick and Amanda seem to think so."

"You don't plan to raise yours here?"

"Are there kids somewhere in the house?" She cast him a glance askance. "I live alone, or didn't you notice?"

Her answer didn't provide the information he was really fishing for. Or explain why she'd smuggled him out of town like a kilo of cocaine across the border. Okay. "Nobody special in your life?"

Her next look held heat. "If there were, do you think I'd have had sex with you on my desk? Or by the waterfall? Or in my bed?" She gripped the steering wheel so hard her fingers whitened. "You have a really low opinion of me."

*Oh, crap.* But he couldn't just say, "I am about to take your town down, want to run away to the big city with me? I'm a celebrity. Why aren't you a fan?"

Of course, if she'd been a fan, she would have recognized him right away. What a mess this was becoming.

"No...I have a high opinion of you. I think you are a smart, beautiful woman with so much to give, it's hard to believe nobody has laid claim to you yet."

Her mouth dropped open, and her voice squeaked. "Claim to me?"

Could he say anything worse? They entered the main highway, and Orlena sped up, driving at least ten miles an hour over the speed limit. He'd be lucky if she didn't just shove him out of the car and leave him for dead. Alden Strong, TV star and charmer of women, was suffering a bad case of diarrhea of the mouth with the first woman who had ever made him want more than a date or two.

# Chapter Six

Orlena leaned heavier on the gas pedal. She wasn't sure what had gone wrong, but, suddenly, Al had become very inquisitive, not to mention insulting. Clearly, he thought she was a tramp. Maybe a tramp who cheated on her "boyfriend" with any guy who came to town. What the hell!

She slowed as she approached the town limits. Officer Tim Hutchins took great pride in adding to the budget with speeding tickets, and she'd already contributed her share. Pulling in by the school, she parked on the side street and turned to face Al. At this point, given a choice, she'd walk away and never see him again. But, with the full moon only hours away, she had to see if the two times she'd let herself go had born fruit.

How stupid could she be? Twice! Her grandmother would have said the second time was accidentally on purpose. But every time he touched her, good sense went out the window. He'd been the one to offer the condoms the other times, or it would have happened again.

Jaw tense, she tried to smile at him. "I have to head to my meeting, but can I meet you at noon at the diner?"

"Great! I will go to my hotel and change then poke around town for a while."

The relief in his face and eagerness in his tone softened her heart a little. And that damn lock of hair falling over his forehead, giving him a little boy vibe that reminded her of one of her naughty students. She never could hold a grudge when they gave her that look.

Glancing around, and seeing no one she knew, she leaned in for a quick peck that turned into a devouring kiss. No little boy here. His tongue stroked hers in a way that sent heat right to her core and made her want to drag him into the backseat and do things that took naughty to a whole new level. Luckily, a corset did not allow that kind of flexibility.

Her cat sent a warning hiss, and she jerked away, scanning the street for the alpha. "I'm going to be late."

They stared at each other, panting a little, and he grinned. "Would that be a tragedy?"

"No, but a sin against the town. This is the most important day of the month in Goldland, and I have to do my part. At least it's not a school day, so I don't have to worry about a bunch of kids in costume. It always makes them antsy."

How she would manage doing her part and watching him for shifting later on, she had no idea. It would involve being in two places at once, more or less.... She would need help.

They parted at the car, he heading downhill to a small B&B on the side street, she to the schoolhouse where town council meetings were held while funds were raised to refurbish their dilapidated city hall. Every time she suffered pangs of guilt over supporting the "hauntings," she thought of her own remodeling project. If the town couldn't afford to pay her teacher's salary, she would just have to watch the Victorian's roof fall in, and that would break her heart.

The day warmed, promising an uncomfortable afternoon in her heavy dress and underthings. Amid clusters of tourists, she climbed the steps to the school and snapped into character, spine straight, shoulders square.

"Hurry now." She clapped her hands. "Class is about to begin."

Dora would conduct a lesson in the morning, and Orlena would do the same in the afternoon. History—the story of the Indigo Princess, the mysterious figure who only deigned to appear once a month, unlike the other, less prominent and realistic ghosts who provided entertainment during the days leading up to and after the full moon.

"Orlena," Tex barked from the principal's office to the left of the front door. She was delighted to notice he had some scratches on his hands—from the scrub at the edge of her property, hopefully. Nosy jerk. "You're late."

She glanced at the old-fashioned wall clock. "Not

quite." Did he know something? He hadn't come close enough to see what she and her guest were up to. She'd know if he had. Focusing on her the rest of the group, she forced a smile. "Everyone ready to begin?"

Tex glared at her, and she wondered how close he had come to the house the night before. It wasn't the first time he'd breached her territory, so she had been annoyed, but not alarmed. She shouldn't let it go on.

Leaning close, she hissed, "Stay out of my range, Tex. This time, I mean it."

"Why, your boyfriend didn't approve?"

*Shit.*

"I don't have a boyfriend, and if I did, he would be none of your business."

"The female alpha is the male's mate." He grasped her wrist when she would have moved away, but she jerked free and bit back her reply. He'd never hidden his interest, but he'd never quite stated it so baldly either, especially in front of the entire council. He considered her his property, whether she agreed or not. She would have to clarify things—but not today. By tomorrow, her "boyfriend" would have moved on, and she'd be alone again. Maybe he wouldn't be so pushy then.

Mayor John Henderson moved to sit behind the big antique desk. "If everyone is ready, we will begin."

Goldland's elder statesman looked to be in his mid-sixties, but he actually had founded the town in 1866, right after the Civil War.

It was one of the best things about their method of creating new shifters. If you wanted a lover, you wanted him or her to live as long as you—and a human who didn't change would age and die long before a shifter lover.

If a pride member was in love with a non-shifter and did his or her best to convince them to become a shifter over a few months with no result, he or she would be encouraged to break up with the person. Whether potential cougars knew what they were signing up for varied—some were told before, others after. There didn't seem to be a perfect solution. Her father had changed her mother, and they'd been inseparable until the mining cave-in that took them away from their children.

She and Tex took seats in folding chairs, along

with the other three members of the town, and pride, council—Emily and Amelia James, old enough to remember the end of the boom, and the saloon owner, Felix Schmidt, an import who had actually come up with the idea that had brought the town back to life and his saloon into prominence.

John banged his gavel—a hunk of silver ore cupped in his palm—onto the desktop. He claimed the new dents caused the antique to become even more valuable, especially since it left traces of silver behind. "I hereby call the meeting to order. As we keep no written records, I won't ask for the minutes."

Emily and Amelia giggled. Which was probably the point. No matter what he did, they behaved like smitten teenagers. They'd gone to school with John, their next-door neighbor for over a century, and rumor had it all three had remained single because he hadn't been able to choose between them.

But then, there were a lot of rumors in a town this small.

"I'll keep this short and sweet because I want all of you out on the street as soon as possible. Last night's events went almost smoothly. The tourists had a good time, and it looks like we will have at least double the number here for the overnight events."

Tex cleared his throat. "I want to report that the 'blip' on the control board has been handled."

"Blip?" What had happened now?

"No big deal, but we had a hysterical tourist because one of the orbs seemed to follow her around the basement of the saloon, and then there was a shriek...."

That was no blip. Tex had a habit of tormenting the most vulnerable tourist who crossed his electronic path. A really irresponsible choice.

"We don't need someone panicking and getting hurt. I thought we agreed, haunting but no terrorizing." She gave him a glare, but his expression radiated innocence.

"Aww, Orlena...." His grin held no guilt. "They come here to be scared."

She shook her head and clasped her hands in her lap. His shenanigans were not her first concern for that particular day. She glanced at the clock. "Is there anything else?"

While John handed out a revised schedule for the

cast members and the various events to be held throughout the day, Orlena tapped her feet quietly under the table, anxious to get moving.

She'd made a second huge mistake at the waterfall. How often could she be irresponsible without repercussions? If it hadn't been effective the first time, what about the second? Shifter 101. A cougar should never have unprotected sex with an ordinary human within twenty-four hours of the full moon. Not unless she wants to take a chance of creating another of her kind. It didn't happen every time, but the odds of missing were not in her favor.

Even though the sun was still climbing in the sky, Al's body might be undergoing the start of the change...and she needed to be close to him as much as she could. Before meeting him for lunch, she needed to grab Dora, fill her in, and swear her to secrecy. The beta's crush on Tex was well-documented, but there was nobody else she could trust, and hopefully her friend could keep her peace for the afternoon. After all, if Al did shift, perhaps there could be more than a one-night stand between them. He would have to stay in town at least for a couple of months until his shifts were under control, and maybe...maybe he'd stay?

One day was not long enough to know if he could be her mate.

Two months might be.

He was the first man in her limited experience who could keep up with her in bed. Her eyes drifted closed at the memory. His hands, his lips, his—

"Adjourned." John brought his gavel rock down with a crunch, and she flinched, eyes open again. Maybe he could be persuaded to use another stone under it next time. Or a tile. One could abuse an antique only so much before making an actual hole in the top. How could that increase its value?

She followed the others into the hallway but lingered as they filed out the front doors. Making a sharp left, she scooted up the stairs and hovered outside the demo classroom. Inside, a few dozen chattering tourists wandered, admiring the historical objects and tintypes displayed around the room. She watched with satisfaction as some slipped cash into the box on the teacher's desk. The school needed some foundation work, and every contribution helped. Finally, the last visitor wandered past her toward the staircase, and she slipped inside.

"Hi there." Dora wore her favorite blue-and-yellow printed calico, a smarter choice than her own heavy sage serge for such a warm day. Her auburn hair, elaborate braids woven into a coiffure that would have made any woman in the 1870s proud, set off her pink cheeks and sea-blue eyes.

How could Tex overlook her? Dora would make the alpha a wonderful, supportive wife, and, despite his claims, the alpha male and alpha female rarely mated. The ways of the heart were beyond her comprehension. Maybe with a loving wife and family, Tex would settle down and put the pride's needs before his own ego. But her own focus on Al bothered her.

Why would she be thinking so much about a man who'd arrived in town yesterday?

One hot night of sex did not a lifetime of wedded bliss make.

A flush of guilt heated her cheeks. One mistake, okay...but the waterfall? Had there been an element of purpose in her actions? She wasn't stupid enough to try to keep him in town against his will. Could she be that pathetically lonely?

She didn't think so. She could decipher her motives tomorrow, after he left.

"Orlena!" Dora said. "Sit right down here and let me do your hair."

She hesitated, but then dropped into the chair. Everything had to be good for the town today. She had to be a femme fatale of a schoolteacher, especially if she intended to keep Al's attention on her until the critical moment. As Dora's gentle fingers loosened her already unraveling plaits and began the process of creating a corona of smooth, perfect braids, suitable for her schoolmarm role, Orlena fidgeted until the other woman stopped and bent to peer at her.

"Okay, out with it. What's up?" Dora's innocent face, long lashes, rosy cheeks, and Cupid's-bow mouth gave her the appearance of a china doll that could have been on the shelf of any little girl long ago. But she was shrewd. While she taught middle-school science, she did it with an MIT degree on her wall. Her presence in town was by choice. She could have gone to work as a chemist in any pharmaceutical house in the country. Tex was her only weak spot.

"I need you to cover for me tonight while I do...while I am onstage." She licked her lips and willed Dora not to ask for more information than she was willing to reveal.

"Sure."

Relief.

"Cover for you, how?"

Well, she would have had to give that info no matter what. "You have to swear you won't tell a soul."

"Of course, you know I've never been a gossip. I'm not going to start now. What's up?"

Orlena felt a little guilty at the ease with which her beloved friend agreed to keep a confidence before she knew what was being asked of her. Friends like that were few and far between. She had one.

"I met a man, and I need you to distract him during my shift." *Shift. God. What a way to put it.*

"Of course, but"—Dora stood and went back to work, coiling braids and pinning them up—"since when do you pick up tourists? What makes this guy special?"

Orlena shrugged. "He's got a hot, sexy body, great in the sack, you know. We spent an amazing night together at my place, and I just don't want him to figure out what we are or, heaven forbid, to attract attention from Tex."

Dora squealed and hopped up to sit on the edge of the desk. "Okay, now I need all the details. He's cute, he's hot, and you *slept* with him? I can't remember the last time you brought anyone home to that shack of yours. Have you ever?"

Orlena scoffed, staring at a sepia photograph of students from long ago. "Of course I have. Remember that guy, Ernie?"

"In college? You weren't even living up there then. You were still at your grandmother's and took him to Tonopah for a weekend of fun." Dora cupped Orlena's chin and forced her to meet her gaze. "And don't try to distract me. Just because you had sex with a guy doesn't mean he's onto what's really going on here, on any level. What did you do?" The color drained from Dora's cheeks. "Oh, my god. You didn't."

Miserable, every bit of glow from the night before

gone, she nodded. "I did."

"Oh, Orlena."

"Twice."

"You had sex twice?"

She shook her head slowly, and Dora's hand dropped away. "About six times, but unprotected, twice."

"Wow." Dora stood and walked toward the window. "Just wow." A long, drawn-out moment passed. "Uh oh, we have bigger problems, look."

Orlena followed her and stared down at the street below.

"What?" All she saw was the thickening crush of welcome tourists, cars and trucks clogging Main Street, and a policeman in period costume directing traffic. Nothing to indicate a bigger problem than the fact she might have turned a stranger into a wildcat.

Dora pointed to the north, just outside the city limits, where several people were spilling out of a white van, carrying cameras and equipment.

Orlena shrugged. "A news crew, so? We get those every month. We do want publicity, right?"

"No, it's not a news crew, and, before you say it,

it's not another ghost-hunting group. There were already a few of those in town before I came in to do my class." Dora flattened her hand against the glass pane then formed a fist. "Look at the side of the thing. It's *Not on My Watch.*

The half dozen men and women, a bunch of hipsters from what Orlena could see, gathered around a man who pointed and gestured, directing them to wherever they would be filming or whatever they were going to do. When they parted, she got a look at him. Tall, lean, wearing a white button-down and jeans that clung to every inch of his delectable butt and legs. His hair caught the sun and shone.

"Hey, that's Al."

Dora groaned. "Al? You mean Alden Strong."

"Who?" She admired the view. Maybe, after lunch, she could get him alone for a few minutes and unbutton that shirt, kiss her way down his—

Her friend grabbed her arm and jerked her to face her. "Alden Strong, the consumer watchdog who has debunked everything from the Scarlet Stalker in Missouri to the headless duke in Buckingham Palace," Dora squeaked. "Why the hell don't you watch television like a normal person?"

"No, he isn't...he can't be. I mean, we spent the night together. We had a picnic by the waterfall." Orlena struggled to draw a breath past the panic rising in her chest and sending her heart thudding into overdrive. "I made pancakes."

"After years of celibacy, you have to find the biggest threat to our welfare, sleep with him, and *turn* him? Why didn't you just get some dynamite out of that mine you love so much and blow up the town?"

"I do love that mine. I'd rather fix Grandma's house with silver than by haunting the halls." She'd never taken a dime for her part in the deceit either—as long as she didn't count the teacher's salary the town probably wouldn't have been able to pay her without it.

"I am not going to discuss your insistence on digging in that dangerous hole in the ground right now." Dora dropped her arm, and they both pressed their foreheads to the warm glass of the window. "But you have made a giant mess, and we need to tell the council."

The group by the van split into pairs and invaded the town. They stopped tourists and costumed townsfolk alike and stuck microphones in their faces. Interviews, she supposed. Had they seen ghosts? Did they believe in them?

*You can call me Al.*

She'd call him more than that.

"Orlena? Let's go talk to Tex or John...or someone."

"No, not yet. I screwed up, and I will fix it."

Dora grimaced. "Okay, but be careful, and if you are in over your head, say so. This is the whole town at stake, not just your love life. After this is over, you need to find a nice cougar guy and settle down."

Not a chance. "After this, I'm done. It's obvious I am not cut out for romance."

"Don't say that."

"Nope." She turned away from the window and gave Dora a hug. "I have my friends and my brother and his family. That will have to suffice. As Grandma Rose always said about Aunt Minnie...I'm a bad picker. Well, she was...but it's the same thing. It's genetic."

She didn't have time to mourn that part of her life. She'd done without sex and romance for a long time, and she could just keep going that way. After taking a moment to loosen the tapes holding her bustle down, she sauntered out of the classroom.

She had a mission—to save the town from those determined to destroy it. Led by a man who, like others in her past, had no trouble deceiving a woman to get into her bed.

Her cat awoke, stretching and purring. *Let's play, kitty. It's always fun to toy with the prey*

# Chapter Seven

"Wait." Alden beckoned his producer back to his side. In their distinctive black shirts, with *NOT,* short for *Not on My Watch,* front and back, hauling cameras and microphones, the crew would stick out like a sore thumb. No more hiding what was going on, but he needed to try to maintain his own anonymity, if he could, for a bit longer. They weren't even supposed to be in town until two.

"I am not going to make a fuss about who I am until after dark. If I'm spotted, fine...but I want you to avoid the schoolmarm in the green dress. Brunette. And don't acknowledge me in public until I give the signal. Let everyone know. Got that?"

Hal lifted an eyebrow. "That's a switch, but sure.

What are you up to?" He winked. "Never mind. None of my business."

Alden gave a brusque nod. "That's right."

"But I'm guessing that may be why you had so little to tell us when we spoke this morning."

At Alden's growl, Hal lifted a hand.

"Calm down. I'll get into town and supervise the troops. You...well, you do whatever it is you are planning to do anyway. But the network won't be happy if they hear you've been deflowering virgin schoolmarms."

*No danger there.* She hadn't been a virgin, although he didn't get the feeling she brought a lot of men home. "Just get going and, remember, you don't know me."

"Until you give the signal, right." He started down the road then paused. "Boss?"

"What now? If you stick around much longer, someone will see us together."

"It's just...." Hal scuffed a shoe in the gravel at the side of the road.

God, would the man never leave? He had to meet Orlena in a few minutes, and he was getting dizzy standing in the sun. "Just, what?"

"Well, we've never had a signal before…so what would that be?" Hal still faced the town, but humor colored his tones and made Alden want to chew nails. And the dumbass was right.

"How about, I just say, 'Hi, Hal'?"

Laughter followed the ruddy-bearded man as he sauntered to town. College roommates made for lousy producers. Well, not true. Hal was brilliant and partly responsible for their success. But he had no fear of the talent—the talent being Alden. His buddy. Hal knew where all the bodies were buried. They'd buried them together.

Not literally.

Locking the van, he wandered toward the diner where he'd agreed to meet Orlena, his steps lightening as he got closer. She'd been so hot in the green dress with his favorite accessory—the bustle— emphasizing her sexy ass. Even though they'd made love five or maybe six times, he was ready to do it again. He hadn't been this randy since college. There was something magic about that woman. He chuckled. If there were any magic. Witches were right up there with ghosts.

Fakery.

Designed to separate a gullible public from their money.

As he approached the center of town, the crowds thickened. Townsfolk in costumes from the period of the silver boom were in each store and restaurant he peeked in, chatting up the visitors, remaining in character.

There was going to be a parade, he understood. At sunset. A young cameraman and his newest crewmember, Sandra, stood outside the diner, interviewing a man in a flannel shirt and dusty trousers with a handlebar moustache and black hair parted and slicked back. He was telling them a long story about the founding of the town. The man had a gift for storytelling, and Alden hoped they were getting some good footage. Sandra's eyes flicked toward him, and he gave her a frown before ducking through the door. He hadn't been undercover once they'd arrived, and it would be a miracle if nobody exposed him before the day ended.

At least, perhaps, he could get through lunch

before someone exposed him.

"Al."

Ah, the sweet tones of his date, waving from a table near the back. Like all the others, it was covered in red-and-white checked oilcloth with a glass pitcher of ice water in the center.

He waved and made his way through the tight press. Every other table was crowded with tourists dining from gold mining pans. Not really authentic, but he supposed they provided atmosphere. Coffee was served in blue enamel mugs, soft drinks in mason jars.

Sliding into the seat opposite her at the two-person table, he momentarily longed for a booth where he might sit closer. "So, what's good here?"

She blinked, her long lashes brushing her cheeks, and a cloud passed over her expression, but a bright smile replaced it. "Well, you are."

He laughed, but something was off. Did she know...had someone told her who he was? She didn't watch television, but she probably had plenty of friends who did.

"Glad to see you, and I return the compliment.

Have you ordered?" With his crew combing the town, it was just a matter of time before someone noticed him. For once, he was glad to sit with his back toward the door—usually, he wanted the comfort of the wall at his back so he could see who was coming and going.

"No, I waited for you. The menu is on the board over the counter, but it's pretty simple. I need to eat and go in kind of a hurry." She lifted a hand. "Crystal, over here."

The waitress couldn't have been more than eighteen or nineteen, and, while she was technically in costume, her blood-red hair, tattooed wrists, and powdered pale skin gave her more of a vampire/goth appearance than an innocent young girl from the Old West. Her maroon dress, heavy with ruffles and off the shoulders, came only to the knee in front, baring black-stockinged legs. Quite a different look from his schoolmarm. And, despite her youth, not nearly so enticing.

"Okay, what will you have?" She was chewing very non-period gum and popping it while she waited...waited.

He glanced over her head. "Burgers good?"

Miss Teen Goth shook her head. "Not really, but they're better than almost everything else."

"And the fries are great," Orlena cut in. "Crystal, you've got to be more positive. Your dad is trying to make a living here."

She rolled her eyes. "Yes, Miss Orlena. I know. But you wouldn't believe some of the freaks that have been in today. I can't wait to get out of this town."

Orlena sucked in a breath and let it out slowly. "Bring us a couple of bison burgers—those really are pretty good—and fries. Iced tea?"

"Sure," he said, realizing the last had been directed to him. "And I have a craving for pie." In his experience, small town diners usually had decent pie.

"Okay, we have apple today." Crystal scribbled their orders on a little pad. "Two apple pies?"

Orlena beamed at him. "Another pie lover."

He smiled back at her, loving the way her eyes sparkled at him. But then another cloud passed. What was she thinking?

"I haven't had pie in ages," he said, "but I'm starving, and it sounded good."

Crystal returned with mason jars filled with iced tea with a wedge of lemon stuck on the side then disappeared, leaving them alone again. He reached for Orlena's hand, but she slid it away and placed it in her lap with the other one. He tried to think how he might have offended her. She couldn't have learned who he was, or she wouldn't be sitting there with him. Or would she? For a moment, he considered telling her. She valued honesty and probably would hate knowing her town deceived people. Maybe she would join him in uncovering the lies.

But how could she not know what was going on? If she believed in ghosts, would she live out there in an old shack more likely to be haunted than the town itself? Wouldn't the winds howling down the canyon in winter scare her? Orlena took a sip of her iced tea and stared down at the glass, turning it as if the secrets to the universe lay in its amber depths.

He sucked in a breath. "So, tell me about the haunting."

Her gaze flicked up to meet his. "What?"

*Interesting reaction.* "Well, I came a long way to see the ghosts. I missed whatever might have happened last night because...." He watched her cheeks flush and plunged on. "Because you were kind enough to invite me to your home. And I don't regret one minute of our time together, but tonight is the big deal, right? The full moon brings out the purple duchess?"

"It's the Indigo Princess."

Like he didn't know. She bit back the words and forced her expression neutral. How dense did he think she was?

"Oh, that's right." He smiled up at Crystal as she placed their plates in front of them. "Full-body apparition seen only on the night of the full moon. I can't wait."

*I'll just bet you can't.* "It's very exciting. I am sure you'll have a great time. Don't miss the parade just after sunset. So colorful." She sounded like the Chamber of Commerce, but in an effort not to call him names or perhaps shift and shred the lying bastard, she had to fall back on something. So, tourism.

"Will you watch it with me?"

"I'm usually in it, but sure, why not? I can probably bow out for once and watch from the sidelines." *Since I have to stick to you like glue every moment I can in case you turn into a mountain lion and try to eat everyone in sight.*

Most shifters weren't nearly so violent, even their first time, but a person's true character tended to reflect in their shifted form, without the civilized veneer. Anyone who could lie like he had might have other flaws. Bad ones. Oh, yeah, she'd skip the parade.

"Great!" He beamed at her without a trace of guile in those blue eyes, and her damn cat purred. She flexed her claws. How could she still like him? Maybe she just wanted a playmate.

*He's nothing to us, kitty. He'll be gone tomorrow.*

Purr.

"Well, eat up," she said, dismissing her cat's disloyalty. "If you want to hear about the hauntings, I will be hosting class time at the school in about a half hour, and I can give you the legend then. It's quite colorful." *Dang, colorful again!*

But her heart hurt too much to be creative. She'd

known him only one day, but somehow his presence had eased her loneliness in a way she'd never have expected. Tomorrow, he'd be gone, or he might be forced to stay, to learn to control his cat—in which case, he'd hate her.

And...what would happen when he went missing? She hadn't counted on him being a national treasure!

She couldn't think about that. If he shifted, she'd have to involve the council, and they would somehow set up a false trail. It had been done before—though not with a celebrity. The weight of her guilt almost strangled her. She'd fought fang and claw against the entire fake haunting and the lies involved, only agreeing when the school was in danger of closing, which would have forced them to bus the children fifty miles each way every day...and she couldn't let that happen.

Now, she'd risked it all. So much for her high morals. Maybe she should tell Tex right away. Even if she were thrown out of the pride for her stupidity and carelessness, they would have a chance to make plans.

But she'd fallen for Al...and if he refused to stay,

what would Tex and his henchmen do?

No, selfish though it might be, she couldn't see him harmed. She'd have to wait, watch closely, and, if all went well, he'd see the show and leave, unscathed and none the wiser. Scanning his face, she saw no signs of any changes, but then why would she? Nothing would show up until the moon rose into the sky.

If anything did at all.

Al—Alden, she reminded herself—lifted his burger and took a big bite. "This is great! I heard buffalo was dry, but it's juicy and delicious. And the fries."

As he waxed enthusiastic about a plate of ordinary diner fare, her worries rose. An increased appetite was certainly an effect of the change, but, then, after the night they'd had, who wouldn't be hungry? Despite her concerns, she gobbled the food, too.

Looking past him, she saw Tex and his second outside, talking with their heads close together. One of those black-T-shirted teams paused to speak to them, but he waved them away, and they didn't press the issue. The girl did cast a glance inside, and her gaze lit on the back of Alden's head. Her boss—but the look on her face said more. A crush? She was awfully young—but didn't TV people sleep around? Approaching thirty, she guessed her lunch companion to be close to her age. Would he have any problem bedding a twenty-year-old?

He'd been fine with jumping the bones of a stranger.

She was a fine one to talk.

Stuffing the last of her burger in her mouth, she waved Crystal over. "Wrap my pie up, would you? I'll eat it after class."

She'd be late in a moment. But she needed to keep him with her—didn't she? Even if nothing happened during daylight, every moment he was with her was one in which he wasn't "investigating" the town. If he found the control room in the basement of the saloon, it would all be over.

"As soon as you're done Ald...Al, I need to get over to the school. If you want to hear the legend, this is your chance."

He shoveled the last bite of pie in, chewed, and swallowed. "Sure. Best meal I've had in years." He grinned at her. "This morning excepted, of course.

I've never had pancakes so delicious."

The sparkle in his eyes made her stomach flip and a crazy thought enter her imagination. Maybe, after class, she could take him into an empty classroom or.... *Stop it!* Crazy ideas got her nowhere. She had responsibilities the rest of the day, and then he'd either leave or hate her or both.

She dabbed her mouth with a napkin and allowed him a smile. If he didn't realize she knew, it would certainly make things easier. So, when he tossed some bills on the table then rose and offered his hand, this time she took it and strolled out of the diner and into the crowded streets of Goldland.

The tourists buzzed along, having a great time. In addition to the unwelcome presence of the *Not on My Watch* gang, she noted T-shirts identifying a few other, more enthusiastic ghost-hunting groups, including one or two making a return visit. The noise level was so high, she longed to hop in her car and head for her canyon, but how ungrateful would that be? Besides, she had no understudy for her singular role in the nighttime festivities.

For the good of the town.... *Just keep saying that*

*over and over*.... She'd repeated that to herself so many times, she almost believed it.

Judging by the number of Indigo Princess hats, shirts, and other paraphernalia, souvenir sales were topping previous records. A percentage of each item sold went to the school—at her insistence.

Alden wrapped his free arm around her waist and tucked her against his side as they threaded through the crowd, and some of her anxiety lessened. The music blasting out of the saloon and every other business added to the chaos, but she fixated on his strength and calmness. He seemed unaffected by the general insanity.

But then he did this sort of thing all the time.

Why did he do it?

What pleasure did he get in ruining the fun of the many people who loved to be scared by harmless hauntings? In stealing the livelihood of small town people just trying to survive? She tried to get really mad—as she should—but the heat of his body sent her own temperature flying. Her nipples peaked under the tight bodice of her dress, and a trickle of moisture traced down her inner thigh before being absorbed by her pantalets.

How could she do what she needed to if he could elicit instant lust like this?

In a desperate attempt to redirect and regain the ire she should rightfully be feeling, she leaned close to his ear and shouted, "So, what do you do, anyway?"

Unfortunately, they reached a less noisy section of the boardwalk just as she spoke, in front of the Cowboy Chapel, and her words carried. A *Not* camera crew member spun to face them and then jerked away again. God, could they be any more obvious? Why was he still carrying on the ruse, anyway? Did he hope to lay her one more time? Or get her to reveal the secrets of the town in a moment of passion? The bastard.

"What time are you due in the schoolhouse?"

"Two," she said, irritated at his redirect. "Why?"

"Because it's five after."

*Shit.* It had taken forever to travel three blocks. She suppressed her annoyance and lifted her skirt, shrugging free of his arm. "Oh, no. Come on, let's get there."

Yet another responsibility she'd allowed him to divert her attention from. Bounding up the steps, she raced inside as fast as her lace-up boots allowed. She'd have blisters from them—but she had those every month. Alden kept up with her, no mean feat, and she paused outside the doorway to catch her breath. Her human self just didn't have the stamina of the cat. Dammit.

She blew out a breath and rested her hand on the jamb. "Just take a seat anywhere and try not to distract me."

His lips curving, he lifted his palm and rested it on her cheek. "I'll do my best, but you're so much fun to distract."

Her breathing sped again, and her heartbeat with it. "Just sit. And don't ask questions."

He traced her lips with his thumb, and she parted them, wanting, wishing for his kiss, trapped in his spell. "You don't allow questions?"

"Yes," she murmured, "just not from you. I have a story to tell."

As the buzz of a full room entered her consciousness, she leaned away, breaking contact with him. There was nowhere for him to sit. The walls were lined with people in shorts and tank tops, even a few non-locals dressed for the 1800s. Every month more of their guests did that, a positive trend.

"I guess you'll have to squeeze in somewhere. Don't leave without me, okay?" *Please.*

"I won't."

As she started to enter, he grabbed her shoulder and dragged her back to him.

"For a kiss." He didn't wait for her answer, just took possession of her lips and devoured every thought she'd had, every bit of anger, of guilt, of weight of responsibility until she forgot where she was or why. He explored her mouth like they had all day, and she let him.

"Orlena!" The bark of the alpha pierced her delicious fog and drove her back to reality. "Orlena, what the hell are you doing?"

"Huh? I'm about to teach my class."

Alden released her, and she stumbled free and scooted through the door, not wanting Tex to interfere in what was going on. He definitely would know who she embraced, and there would be repercussions, but not right now. Not at that moment. She'd deal afterward.

As she took her place at the front of the room, and the visitors stilled, focusing on her, she could hear a murmur of low conversation in the hallway. Then Alden slipped inside and found a piece of wall to occupy. What had Tex said? What would he say to her when he got her alone? She'd have to make sure that didn't happen until tomorrow because today she had more than enough to deal with.

"Good afternoon, class." She began her prepared lesson, forcing a smile on her face and patting her hair to make sure it was all in place. "I am Miss Orlena, and today I have a very special story to tell you. It's a history lesson about something that happened right here in Goldland. Has anyone heard the legend of the Indigo Princess?"

## Chapter Eight

Alden leaned against the wall, his gaze on nothing but the woman who had thrown him so far off track. He had crews wandering the streets of a ghost town doing their jobs while he stood in a classroom and waited for her to tell him a story.

At least he saw one of his crews over by the windows, recording the session. When he debunked the hauntings, the telling of the legend behind it would be a compelling portion of the show. And he would be able to play it over and over, the second and last day Orlena Estelle was willing to give him her time, her kisses, her friendship. It would never move beyond that. When she realized his purpose, even if she was an innocent in the deceit, she would never be able to forgive him for helping to kill her home.

Generations of her family had dwelled there, mined for silver, and occupied the Victorian right on Main Street. And he, Alden Strong, would be solely responsible for making it a different kind of ghost town.

But, once she began to speak, all he could do was listen, as enraptured as the rest.

"The Indigo Princess is not only the name of the first mine in Goldland where silver was discovered." She smiled. "Did you know that there has never been any gold here? Just silver. But the first people in town were looking for gold."

"It should be Silverland, then," a voice piped up. His crewmember, Sandra. He was running into her far too often for coincidence and would have to be sure she understood there would be nothing between them but business.

"You're right. But...it is what it is, and we're all used to it, so Goldland it was and Goldland it shall remain. Once upon a time.... I think all stories, even true ones, should begin that way, don't you?"

Orlena was mesmerizing.

"Once upon a time, a handsome miner came to town to sell his ore. He was very excited about his finds because he had worked hard for years and believed he could succeed. Even though nobody else thought he could. He never gave up his dreams. He sang as he traveled out of the mountains and along the dirt track. There were no highways in those days, so it was a long and bumpy ride."

The classroom melted away, and Alden became lost in the world she created.

"As he rode past the saloon, he saw a heavyset man with a florid complexion arguing with a woman. He'd never seen such a beautiful lady before or one so exotic. Her black hair was like silk, falling free past her waist, and her eyes were tipped at the corners but swimming with tears. She tried to pull away, but the man held tight to her wrist and slapped her across the face. 'You belong to me, and I will do what I want with you.' He slapped her again, and her head snapped back. 'And I want you to go in there and service those men, make me some money. You're eating me out of house and home.'

"The miner slowed his horse. He didn't like to get

between a man and his woman—it was an excellent way to get shot in those days—but he didn't like to see anyone mistreated either. Or accused of eating too much when she looked so thin. He worried she didn't get half enough to eat. And her dirty, torn purple-blue dress stood in stark contrast to the man's fancy clothes. Like she'd been in the same outfit for some time with nothing to change into.

"Trying not to attract attention, he slid from his horse and tied it to the rail in front of the saloon. He fussed with the saddlebags while waiting to see what would happen next. What did he mean the woman belonged to him? Was she his wife? Because, at that time in the United States of America, slavery had finally been outlawed.

"The lady fell to her knees in the dust of the street. 'I will not,' she said. 'If I do as you ask, I might as well be dead. Please let me go.'

"The man drew his hand back again, and the miner moved in. Seeing a woman abused was more than he could bear, and he closed his fist around the man's arm and punched him in the jaw.

"The lady covered her face with her hands,

sobbing, and the miner helped her to her feet. 'Ma'am, what is that man to you? Is he your husband?'

"She shook her head, tears pouring down her cheeks in a deluge. 'I am, or was, an amah to a British family newly arrived in the town of Reno, and I was on my way to the market when he scooped me up and rode away. I've been sleeping tied to him for weeks because he feared I would run. And I would have, or killed myself, if I'd had the weapons.'

"The miner glared down at the man, unconscious at his feet, and gave him a good kick. He offered to take the lady to her employer, but she begged him not to, to keep her with him. She could not return and had nowhere else to go. She pled with him not to tell the sheriff of the man's crimes, as she didn't want word of her dishonor to get back to the family she had worked for. They would have returned her to India, where the shame of the tale would kill her mother. Completely smitten by her beauty and gentle spirit, the miner helped her onto his horse and, with only one quick stop, carried his new wife off to his mine in the mountains. He kept watch for the man, but, when weeks then months passed with no sign of him, they became sure he'd moved on to another place.

"Among the trees and the waterfalls, the lady healed from her wounds, her bruises, and the horrors she'd experienced while in the clutches of the evil man. And, in time, she gave her husband a baby, a little girl they named Aspen for the trees the lady had grown to love. She'd reached paradise and found love at the mine called the Indigo Princess. For, you see, she admitted to her husband that she was, in truth, of royal blood and had taken the job with the family leaving India in order to escape a marriage she did not want and could not accept."

Orlena stood in front of her desk as she spoke, with the posture of a princess, and, now that he knew the story, Alden could see in her straight hair and dark eyes a bit of her Indian heritage. She spoke of her home, of the mine, of her great-grandfather, and of her great-grandmother. He held no doubts that she was the great-granddaughter of the Indigo Princess.

She gazed off into the distance above their heads. "One day, while the miner was off at his labors, deep in the earth, and the baby, Aspen, slept in her cradle, hoofbeats sounded outside the little shack. The lady peeked out the window and saw her greatest nightmare. The man who had stolen her once had tracked her down. Before she could grab for the rifle hung over the door, he was inside and had a pistol pointed at her stomach, where a new infant grew.

"He ordered her to come with him, and she refused. They argued. But then the baby made a sound, and he smiled. A smile so evil it chilled her blood. 'A baby. Is it mine?'

"'No, if I had found myself with your spawn, I would have killed myself,' she cried.

"'Then I have no reason to let it live.'

"She fell to her knees and wailed, and he smiled with all the evil he possessed. 'Then you may, if you ask nicely, come away with me. If I do not find your begging pleasing, I will kill your child, and then I will find the man who gave you that child and kill him, too.' Her miner might be able to defend himself, unless the evil man snuck up on him, but the baby had nobody to protect her except her mother so, sobbing, she packed a bag and allowed the man to lead her away. She closed the door tight so no animals could get in before the baby's father returned from work. It was the only gift she could give her daughter.

"She would have to try and save herself and the new life within her as best she could."

Orlena paused, seemingly lost in the far-off past. Her eyes mirrored the light, and she continued. "The miner returned to find a screaming, hungry baby and no sign of his beloved wife. Though he searched for many years, while his daughter became a woman and he grew old, he never learned what happened to her. But it is said that, on the night of the full moon, she returns to haunt the town where nobody but a lonely miner could be bothered to save her from an evil so great, it finally consumed her life."

The silence held for a long moment before the questions started, but Orlena...Miss Orlena...clapped and then crossed her arms. She leveled a teacher stare that would have done the nuns at Saint I-Can't-Believe-I-Went-To-Catholic-School proud and, in under a minute, the room was quiet again. "One at a time, please. Raise your hands if you would like to be heard."

One after another, she answered them with great poise. No, there had been no sign of the lady ever again, but, a while back, a pair of skeletal remains had been found in the desert. The coroner had determined they were over a hundred years old but could not identify the cause of death. The skeletons were eventually returned to town, and DNA from a descendant of the woman had determined her identity. The other was male, but unidentified. They had died of gunshot wounds in the desert.

Despite her tale-telling ability, a big question remained in his mind and in the mind of at least one other.

Orlena called on a big fellow in biker gear.

"If she never returned and nobody ever saw her again...how do we know she didn't just leave with her former lover of her own free will? They could have been killed by robbers...or even the miner if he caught up with them."

The women in the crowd glowered at him.

"He had abused her," hissed a middle-aged housewife type.

"It wouldn't be the first time a woman returned to her abuser." The guy in leathers shrugged. "Happens all the time."

As the schoolmarm paced down the aisle to where the big, bearded fellow overflowed a desk, Alden was grateful he hadn't been the one to pose the question—although he wouldn't have taken it that far. Still, the man had a point.

"My great-grandmother would not have done that. She loved her family and her home at the Indigo Princess Mine."

Her great-grandmother. When she said it like that, with the full force of her considerable personality behind it, the big bad biker shrank back in his seat, and the woman who had confronted him smiled.

The guy didn't ask any more questions, but Orlena rested her hand on his shoulder and offered an angelic smile to the rest of the group. "Although it was asked in a less-than-genteel way, this gentleman asked a valid question. If you go to the saloon later this afternoon, you will find, framed and mounted on the wall behind the bar, the letter my great-grandmother left behind when she packed her bag.

Rather, a copy. The original is locked away in a vault, as it is extremely important to my family.

"And every month, on the night of the full moon, the Indigo Princess—for, you see, we have learned that the amah was in truth of ancient royalty—runs away from a marriage she didn't want.

"Now, if there are no more questions, I know you will all want to go see the letter and maybe have some refreshments before the parade after sundown. Our townspeople are most gracious, and the locals in costume have their own tales to tell you." Giving a squeeze, she let the frozen biker go. "Just ask."

When Orlena returned to sit at her desk, the people began to file out. A few stopped to speak with her, but most were heading for the saloon to see the letter. They chattered about it as they passed him, so excited to see even a copy of such an important artifact.

When the room emptied, he drifted toward her, and she lifted her face to him. "So, how did you like the story?"

"I liked how you told it." He rested a hip on the desk.

"What's the matter, don't you believe it?"

He cocked his head and looked at her, seeing the Indian girl in her straight brows and dark brown eyes. "No, I believe you had a great-grandmother who came from India." His research team hadn't indicated there was a living descendant. He'd have to make sure that kind of slipup didn't occur again. "And I believe she was of royal blood."

"So, what don't you believe?"

He considered his words. "I don't believe in ghosts."

Her eyes narrowed, and she rose. "Come on. I need to be out and about on the street for the afternoon." Taking his arm, she closed her fingers until they dug into his elbow, and he wondered if she intended to hurt him. "What is it you do for a living, anyway, *Al*. You've never actually said."

And he didn't intend to. "No, I guess I didn't. Right now, I am spending the day out of time with a gorgeous woman from 1870, and I don't want real life to intrude." True that.

Her troubled gaze met his as they descended the staircase. "But it always does, doesn't it? Could you see yourself living in a town like this? Never sure there will be enough money to pay the bills, always struggling a little, worried about your neighbor's kids being bussed far away on snowy roads in winter because the town can't pay the teacher?"

He shook his head. "Never given anything like that any thought. It would be a real problem."

"Yes," she murmured. "But not yours."

# Chapter Nine

Not his problem in the slightest. The remainder of the afternoon passed while Orlena moved from place to place in town, talking to people, answering their questions, sharing parts of the Indigo Princess's story, and keeping an eye on Alden. He remained silent, for the most part, hanging back while she played her teacher's role, bringing her water from time to time and urging her to sit in the shade when she got a little dizzy from the heat.

A nice guy, a caring guy.

A guy out to ruin the town.

And he knew only about one issue. So far.

She'd noticed his skin felt a little warmer, closer to her own temperature, when he took her hand to lead her to sit down. Could be a result of the afternoon's heat.

Or not.

As the sun dipped toward the horizon, she watched him closer. Looking for signs. She couldn't afford to miss them. He shouldn't change until sometime after nightfall, probably close to midnight his first time. Long after the parade and the other shenanigans, including hers. He would despise her if he learned she played such a significant role in the show that was the Indigo Princess.

She stood by his side as the parade passed. It was more historical than anything, with some lights flickering for atmosphere. The townsfolk didn't want to imply that they were the spooks. But, as the sky darkened and lights flickered on in the various businesses, she knew the special effects had also begun. A group of teenage girls came shrieking out of the diner where mysterious forces would have sent empty pie pans clattering to the floor in full view. In the schoolhouse, a light moved from window to window. Orbs would be passing through other places and strange electronic noise that those who had "ghost hunting" equipment would translate to suit their own desires.

Fun. Fun Fun.

They encountered Dora outside the saloon. She was out of breath. "Oh, good. I didn't know where you were. Orlena, Tex would like to speak to you for a few minutes." They probably should have made more specific plans. Lucky her friend kept her head about her, even if she herself was more interested in the body and mind of the man about to destroy them all if he could.

Or whose life she was going to rip open. His fingers were still hot, even after the sun had long disappeared.

"Oh, thanks. Al, this is my friend Dora." She extricated her hand from his. "Dora, would you keep Al company while I track down Tex and see what he needs? I hope it won't take too long, but it's hard to get through this crowd."

"Sure, Orlena." Dora slipped between them and smiled up at Alden from her diminutive height of five foot nothing. "Maybe we'll go get something to drink at the diner." Good plan since that would keep him far from her while she did her ghostly duties.

Waving, she slipped into the crowd and around the back of the saloon. Since Felix had been the one to supply the funding for the initial hauntings, he had insisted that the full-body apparition of the Indigo Princess make her appearance on his premises. She'd argued that if there were anywhere her great-grandmother would have wanted to avoid, it would have been the place her captor had been trying to drag her, but to no avail.

Her costume—an indigo silk dress with one artful tear and a long black wig—was hung in the basement, in a small dressing room next to the control room, and she quickly slipped into the ensemble, hating herself for it. Tex sat at the board when she emerged, manipulating events occurring throughout Goldland. They would go on all night, but she would make only one appearance.

"Ready?" He kept his head bent over his board, but his anger vibrated his voice. "Or have you already spilled all our secrets to that TV guy?"

She adjusted the waistline of her dress and smoothed the skirts. "Of course I haven't told him anything. I didn't even know who he was until almost noon, you know. I don't watch television."

He glanced over his shoulder and sneered. "Right. Too good for TV, too good for me. I get it."

Orlena moved to the foot of the stairs. "We don't have time for this conversation right now."

"No," he said, flicking switches. "We don't. But we will tomorrow. I'm calling an emergency council meeting to discuss your pride membership. You've endangered us by this behavior, and I am thinking maybe it's time for you to move on."

She gaped. "Move on? Tex, I live here. I own property, and my family has been in the pride for three generations, ever since my great-grandfather left his pride in Pennsylvania to mine out here. You can't just throw me out. I have a vote in this."

What would she do, where would she go? They couldn't actually take away her land, but they could harass her until she gave up and left. Would her friends do that? It wouldn't be the first time, and, while she hadn't participated in the actual harassment of others, she hadn't done anything to stop it, either.

How ironic.

"If you do that, who will be the princess in your little show?"

He shrugged. "With the wig? Almost anyone. Even Dora, although she's a little short for the role."

"This isn't over, Tex." She climbed a couple of steps. "You are just angry because you want me for yourself."

Without warning, he jumped to his feet and was at her side. He yanked her down from the steps and, with a hand at the nape of her neck, dragged her against him, knocking her wig askew. Orlena struggled, but he was at least as strong as her and had the element of surprise.

"Let me go, right now." Panic swirled in her brain. "I'll scream."

He bared his teeth in a terrifying rictus of a smile. "Good. The tourists will love it. One more ghost shrieking in the night. In fact...." He kissed her, grinding his lips onto hers and acid filled her throat. "Maybe I will just exercise my rights as alpha and make you my mate tonight."

"What about my appearance?"

"I'll use the holographic backup. It's not as good, but it will work. I'll set it up now."

Backing up to sit in the chair at the controls, he pulled her onto his lap. "We can't have an alpha female who shows such bad judgment, can we?" He tossed the wig aside.

As Tex worked the hologram section, she tried to stand, but he wrapped one arm around her waist and held her firm

"Let me go right now, Tex."

"You need someone to take you in hand, Orlena— you belong to me."

Rage and fear rolled into one and reminded her who she was. Not her great-grandmother without the ability to defend herself.

No, she was a great mountain cat. And she belonged to *herself*.

Her cat roared and poured forth, shifting her to the deep golden being who could defend herself against anything and anyone. With a snarl, she faced him, claws extended.

Tex followed, leaping in front of them and, bones cracking, changed into his cat form, paler yellow with piercing green eyes. He crouched to pounce, just as the door crashed open.

Alden stood in the doorway, Dora behind him.

"I tried to stop them. I—"

But Alden pushed Dora away and stood in front of her, arms extended.

"Oh, my God. There are two mountain lions down there."

"Cougars."

"Go get help, Dora." He dragged on the door, but his entrance had broken so many of the old boards, it splintered under his touch. "Clear the saloon before someone gets hurt."

Orlena's cat still snarled at Tex, but the other cougar padded toward the stairs, his intent clear. Why didn't Dora get Alden out of there?

She leapt and landed on his back, bringing him down, and they rolled, snarling, biting, and clawing. As the anger and hatred of both herself and her cat surged, she sank her teeth into Tex's shoulder, grappling with him, desperate to keep him from getting free and going after Alden. He flung her off and attacked again, fangs piercing her hindquarters and dropping her to the floor. Blood flowed from the wound, and she was unable to rise on her damaged leg.

Tex released her and drew back. She panted and waited for the killing blow.

A golden blur fell on him, and, before she could take in what happened, Tex lay bleeding out, his jugular ripped open by the biggest cat she'd ever seen. One with blue eyes. The council crowded the top of the stairs, watching, but taking no action.

Within minutes of shifting, Alden had challenged and bested the alpha.

And saved her.

She nuzzled him and padded toward the back entrance, away from the crowds. The mayor could handle the rest of the night, including the special effects and the disposal of the former alpha's body.

For now, she would take Alden home. And try to explain. Alden was not an out-of-control animal and could make his own decisions, but he would need all the facts. He was the new alpha.

And, when he turned those strange blue cat's eyes on her, they held fire and love and the gleam of her mate.

She'd never seen this coming.

# Epilogue

"The view never gets old." Alden steered the Snowcat up the track while she held onto his waist. "I think I like it even better in winter."

"It's beautiful." Orlena squeezed him tighter, savoring his heat and nearness. "I only wish you didn't have to go away so often."

"It's only for a while longer," he said, a familiar refrain. "And I think it's important that I don't live off my woman's silver mining and teaching income."

Alden had taken control of the pride as if he'd always been one of them, but had nothing to do with the business of haunting. He refused to even discuss the new angry male spirit who had taken the place of the Indigo Princess the last two full moons. Orlena was very happy to keep her end of the deal—she'd never liked being a ghost anyway.

The network loved that he lived in the one town he'd failed to debunk...a fact that appeared in every article about Goldland—many framed on the walls of the saloon.

Alden had begun traveling between work and their home in the mountains. The Victorian, which his salary would turn into a showplace, would make a suitable home for the alpha male and female of the pride. It also helped that he'd negotiated a new reality show, which would film only a few months of the year and not keep him away from his new responsibilities as much. In fact, since it focused on vacation scams, its summer filming time would enable his wife and baby to travel with him.

Her great-grandmother had been saved by a stranger, but her life had been cut short. No one was even sure if she'd become a shifter before her death. Orlena's attacker would not come back to hurt her, although rumors of a new, angry male spirit attracted more tourists than ever.

They drew up in front of the shack, and he slid off

the seat and shifted, flying ahead of her up the path, eager as always to reclaim their territory after time away. Orlena shifted, following the big cat to their special place. The place she'd spent that first night with him while he adjusted to his cat form. Where she'd confessed her fault at changing his life without his say-so and where he'd claimed her—after he'd recovered his human form—as his mate.

Orlena bounded over the snow, her paws kicking up clouds of the white stuff. How times changed.

She would wait until they reached the warm waterfall to give him her news. Their two oopses a few months before had born more fruit than he knew. For the first time in a long time, new life would grace the shack below the mine.

The Indigo Princess would approve.

# About the Author

Kate Richards is a multi-published author of spicy romance stories in various subgenres. She lives in sunny Southern California with her wonderful husband and menagerie of rescued pets.

Kate loves the beaches, mountains and deserts of her home state as well as traveling whenever possible to meet readers and other authors.

Exploring all types of relationships in her books, Kate writes menage, BDSM, and every other kind of romance she can think of.

# Other Titles by Kate Richards

One Night on the Beach

Avalon for Christmas

The Virgin and the Playboy

The Virgin and the Best Man

Two Men and a Virgin

Gale Force Passion

Trail of Hearts

Madame Eve's Gift

Two Men

Virgin Underground

Two Dads for Christmas

The Milkman Cometh

Frontier Inferno

Lily in Chains

Terci in Chains

Sweet Christmas Kisses

All's Fair